Cleared for Takeoff

Cleared FOR Takeoff

Fifty Ways Parents Can Help Teenagers
Grow Up and into Lives of Their Own

Wayne Rice
Drawings by Dan Pegoda

WORD PUBLISHING
NASHVILLE
A Thomas Nelson Company

Library of Congress Cataloging-in-Publication Data

Rice, Wayne.
    Cleared for takeoff / by Wayne Rice.
      p. cm.
    ISBN 0-8499-4201-2 (tp)
    1. Parenting—Religious aspects—Christianity. 2. Teenagers—Religious life.
    I. Title.
BV4529 .R52 2000
248.8'45—dc21   00-036484

Printed in the United States of America

00 01 02 03 04 05 PHX 9 8 7 6 5 4 3 2 1

Contents

Contents

Introduction

The two most important things parents can give their kids are roots and wings.

W*hen are you going to start acting your age?* Tough question. Your teenager probably responds about the same way you did at that age—with a shrug of the shoulders and a blank look of helplessness and frustration. This is inevitably followed by another fruitless lecture on growing up, being responsible, *thinking* before acting, behaving oneself, showing a little consideration, and countless other admonitions which go in one ear and out the other.

All parents since Adam and Eve have harbored serious doubts about their offspring's ability to become a responsible, self-reliant adult. For many parents today, those doubts have turned to sheer panic. They just can't imagine their children surviving on their own in the real world. Do you sometimes worry that *your* teenager may never leave home?

No question about it. It's harder for kids to grow up in today's world. It takes longer for today's "millennial kids" to find their way to adulthood than it did for us or for our ancestors.

There was a time when almost all young people claimed their adulthood by the age of eighteen or, at the latest, twenty-one. Now, it's not uncommon to find young adults living at home, hanging out and partying with their friends, acting and looking like, well, *teenagers*, until their thirtieth birthday and beyond. They postpone for as long as possible such adult responsibilities as choosing a career, finding a mate, or becoming financially independent. One of today's trendy lifestyle choices is to avoid adulthood for as long as you can. The new term used to describe this demographic group is *adultescents*.

About twenty-five years ago, researchers studied a sample of high-school students from around the country and found that four years after graduation, 25 percent of them were still living with their parents. Fourteen years later, the same researchers repeated their study and this time found that nearly 50 percent were still single and living with their parents. Is this a continuing trend? It's hard to say, but there's no question that it's more difficult for today's kids to emancipate themselves from their parents than it was for generations of the past.

This of course can be troubling to a parent, given that one of the goals of parenting is to *work yourself out of a job*. You really don't want to parent your children forever . . . do you? Sooner or later, your kids need to grow up, leave the nest, and start living independently and responsibly. Your kids need to be weaned—which has never been easy for either the *weaner* or the *weanee*.

Why is it harder for kids to become adults today?

Primarily because they aren't expected to. Whereas youths of the past were considered adults shortly after reaching physical maturity (puberty), today's young people are relegated to that never-never land called *adolescence*, a kind of staging area for adulthood where they remain for ten years or more.

This is a relatively new development in human history. Prior to the twentieth century, there were only two stages of life—childhood and adulthood. But now there are three—childhood, adolescence, and adulthood. Adolescence has even been divided into three more stages: early adolescence, middle adolescence, and late adolescence. The invention of adolescence in 1904 by the famous psychologist G. S. Hall ultimately gave impetus to the astounding rise of youth culture as we know it today with its own distinctive language, music, and lifestyle.

That's why the Bible offers so little help on raising teenagers. Teenagers simply didn't exist in Bible times. There were teens, of course, but they were considered young adults. In fact, the word that is usually translated *youth* in the Bible actually means young man or young woman.

In the days when American children attended one-room schoolhouses, it was common for students to complete their education before the teen years and begin working on the family farm or in the family business as soon as they were capable. Children became adults probably more out of necessity than anything else. Higher education was only for those who were gifted or who were pursuing careers in fields like medicine, law, or religion.

We can be thankful that today's youth are much better educated than ever before (a necessity in today's complicated high-tech world), but this has resulted in the unfortunate postponement of adulthood. And in turn, today's youth are more likely to remain isolated from their elders until they are well into their adult years. Adults generally feel alienated from youth because they believe that adolescents are not like them and don't want them around. Thus, teens and adults tend to avoid each other—resulting in a loss of mentoring which could help young people make a smooth transition out of adolescence. It has also resulted in the increased vulnerability of today's youth to all sorts of negative and self-destructive behaviors.

Sooner or later, all children eventually grow up to become adults. For some, the process is difficult and dangerous; for others, it's relatively smooth. One thing is certain: If kids have parents who are there for them and who will encourage them on their journey, they will more than likely take flight without having to be pushed out of the nest or without crash-landing.

It has been said that the two most important things parents can give their kids are roots and wings. In this book I offer a list of fifty ways to give your kids the wings they need to fly out of your life and into successful lives of their own. This is the ultimate goal of parenting. Contrary to popular opinion, parents who have become "empty nesters" don't need sympathy or therapy, but congratulations.

Our goal as parents is to get our kids into adulthood with the skills they need to survive on their own and with the self-confidence and resourcefulness to be productive on their own. The process of raising kids well is called "habilitation," because it makes *rehabilitation* unnecessary. If we do our jobs reasonably well as parents, our kids will reach adulthood without having to catch up or recover what they failed to get when they were younger.

Children turn into adults with or without your help. You can't postpone their growing up until it's more convenient. It's going to happen, probably before you are ready. The purpose of this book is to help you become a parent who is involved—an active parent—so that your teenager will have the best chance to grow up and develop strong wings.

Keep in mind that there really are no simple answers to successfully helping teenagers mature into solid, productive, well-adjusted adults. The concepts in this book should be regarded as principles, guidelines, and ideas from one parent to another. Most of it is common sense—stuff you already know. But it's good to be reminded periodically of what we already know.

This is not a psychology book or a book written by a parenting expert. An expert in this field is usually a person who never lived with a teenager or who parented one so long ago he or she has conveniently forgotten everything but what worked. I am only an expert at raising my own three children who are now grown up and gone. Nobody is an expert at raising *your* kids. Every child is unique, as is every family. Some kids mature quite naturally on their own without a lot of coaching from the sidelines; others require an enormous amount of attention, guidance, and discipline.

Parenting isn't always easy, but it's certainly not rocket science. You already know most of what you need to know to help your teenager grow up. This book has been written primarily to serve as an encouragement to you in the important role that you play in the life of your young adult child—your teenager.

Raise an Eagle,
Not a Prairie Chicken

If you want to end up with an adult, then you'll need to raise one.

O nce upon a time there was a prairie chicken that found an egg and sat on it until it hatched. Unbeknownst to the prairie chicken, the egg wasn't a prairie chicken egg; it was an eagle egg. For some reason the egg had been abandoned, so a baby eagle was born into a family of prairie chickens.

Now while the eagle is the greatest of all birds, soaring majestically above the heights with grace and ease, the prairie chicken doesn't even know how to fly. In fact, prairie chickens are so lowly that they eat garbage.

Predictably, the little eagle, being raised by prairie chickens, grew up thinking he was a prairie chicken. He waddled around, ate garbage, and clucked like a prairie chicken.

Then one day, he looked up and saw a beautiful eagle soaring through the sky, dipping and turning. He asked what it was, and his prairie chicken family said, "It's an eagle. But you could never be like that because you are just a prairie chicken." The little eagle spent his whole life looking up at eagles, longing to join them among the clouds. It never once occurred to him to spread his wings and fly.

◆ ◆ ◆

Today's young people are a lot like that prairie chicken. They may have adult bodies, adult brains, and adult aspirations, but they are told that they aren't adults at all. "You're just a teenager" is what they hear, and because they hear it so many times for so many years, they resign themselves to pecking the

1

ground and eating garbage. It never once occurs to them to spread their wings and fly.

Are you raising an eagle or a prairie chicken—an adult or a teenager? This is an important question for parents to consider. Why? Because *if you are raising a teenager, that's more than likely what you'll end up with—a teenager.* Teenagers don't magically turn into adults on their twenty-first birthday.

Conversely, if you want to end up with an adult, then you'll need to raise one. The first step toward that end is to start thinking of your adolescent son or daughter as a *young adult-in-training.* In reality, the only difference between a teenager and an adult is experience (or lack of it). What teenagers need are experiences that will prepare them adequately for adulthood and mentoring from parents and adults who will encourage them and guide them along their way.

Like the prairie chicken in our story, kids need a clear and accurate understanding of who they are and what they will someday become. Not surprisingly, parents are like mirrors where kids see their identities reflected most clearly. When they have parents who believe in them and expect them to fly—to reach the heights of their potential—they will believe it also, for as a person thinks in his heart, so he is (see Proverbs 23:7). Every child was created in God's image and gifted by Him to achieve extraordinary things—to *soar like an eagle* (see Isaiah 40:31). It's unfortunate that so many kids today are led to believe they are nothing but prairie chickens.

Begin with the End in Mind

If you want to help your kids grow up and into lives of their own, then you'll need to practice long-range parenting. It's easy to get so wrapped up in the day-to-day hassles of family life that you don't stop to consider the ultimate objective of parenting—which is to raise healthy, self-reliant adults, not to have a house full of obedient children.

It's clear from Scripture that God has a long-term perspective for our kids. We may not be able to see the big picture, the finished product, but God can. Even while your kids were in the womb, God had big plans for them (see Isaiah 49:5; Jeremiah 1:5). Did you? Probably not. We don't usually think that far ahead. When a baby is born, the doctor doesn't announce, "Congratulations, you've just given birth to a future university professor." That might be nice to hear, but all we really care about is whether the baby is normal and healthy.

At some point, however, it's important to "set our eyes on the prize," as the old saying goes, to remember that our goal, our responsibility, is to raise kids to adulthood. Have you thought about your goal as a parent? Goal setting is a universally accepted principle of effective leadership that certainly has an application to parenting. In other words, if you don't know what you are trying to accomplish, then you probably won't get it done.

Dream a little bit for your teenager. What kind of person do you want your son or daughter to become? Certainly you have no way of predicting exactly how your kids are going to turn out because every person is an individual who must ultimately decide for himself what he wants to be and do.

Still, as a parent, you can set some goals for yourself and for your kids. This will provide them with a kind of road map for their lives, and it will also help you as a parent to guide and encourage your kids along that path. You may not be able to control all that your child does, but you can most certainly control what you do. That's the purpose for setting goals for your kids. Parents play a huge role in the development of children, and those who understand that from the beginning will be in the best position to see their hopes and dreams for their kids become a reality.

An Example from the Bible

Want a worthy goal for your kids? Look no further than Luke 2:52. In this verse, we are given a summary glimpse into the adolescence of Jesus, who "grew in wisdom and stature, and in favor with God and men." From this verse we learn that Jesus matured in every area of His life—the intellectual (wisdom), the physical (stature), the spiritual (in favor with God), and the social (in favor with men). Isn't this how you would like your son or daughter to grow up? Substitute your own child's name in that verse: "And _____ grew in wisdom and stature, and in favor with God and men." Wouldn't you like to be able to say that someday about your kids?

I believe you can. That verse isn't out of the realm of possibility for your kids. Jesus was a teenager, just like yours are. He was *fully human* as the

Apostle's Creed puts it, and all of us are encouraged as His followers to imitate Him.

How did Jesus grow up to become such a fine young man? The Gospels don't give us many details about Jesus' adolescent years, but we do get a clue in verse 51: "[Jesus] went down to Nazareth with them [his parents] and was obedient to them." Mary and Joseph were obviously very good parents. Can you imagine setting limits and providing discipline for the Son of God? But they did what all good parents must do—they were actively involved in raising their son to manhood. They knew what He would someday become, and they never stopped believing in Him. God trusted Mary and Joseph with His only Son.

And God has trusted you with your kids. They are His, but He has given you the responsibility to help them become what He created them to be. While you cannot control every aspect or outcome of your teenager's life, you can provide appropriate amounts of encouragement and influence. Despite rumors to the contrary, parents remain the most important factor in how kids turn out. While there are no guarantees or magic formulas for raising good kids, your efforts to be a good parent will pay off.

Look into the Future

If you want to get a little more specific, you might find it worthwhile to actually sit down and write out your parenting goals. Refer to the Sample Parenting Goal included in this chapter for ideas. What qualities of character do you believe are important? What kind of person do you want him or her to become? Write those things down and commit yourself to doing all you can to encourage and inspire your son or daughter in those areas. Use what you have written as a reminder to hang in there, even when things aren't going so smoothly. Don't use it as a reminder to yourself (or your kids) of how far they still have to go. That will only frustrate everybody. But if you have a mental picture of the kind of people you want your kids to become, and treat them accordingly, there's a good chance they may live up to your expectations.

A true story: A four-year-old girl named Cheryl hung out at her father's small country grocery store. Almost daily, the milkman would come into the store with his delivery and greet her with the words, "Good morning,

Cheryl. How's my little Miss America?" At first she giggled when he would call her that—but over time, she grew comfortable with it, even liked it a little. Soon the milkman's greeting became a childhood fantasy . . . then a teenage dream . . . then a young woman's goal . . . and a few years later . . . Cheryl Prewitt stood on a stage in Atlantic City and was crowned Miss America, 1980.

Even a milkman can give a young child the dream that may someday become a reality. What dream can you give yours? Will your kids become eagles or prairie chickens? If you believe in your kids and let them know you do, don't be surprised to look up one day and find them soaring.

A SAMPLE PARENTING GOAL

We the parents of Kyle Jeffrey Meadows pledge ourselves to help him grow up to become a capable, independent, and godly man . . .

∗ who will be able to make wise decisions based on sound principles,

∗ who will be emotionally and spiritually strong,

∗ who will enter into healthy relationships with other people,

∗ who will be able to accept responsibility for himself, his family, and his vocation,

∗ who will be able to overcome difficult times with perseverance and grace,

∗ who, if he marries, will be a faithful and loving husband and parent,

∗ who will glorify God in his work and his service to others.

Build a Strong Nest

All things are created twice.

Have you ever looked closely at a bird nest? Usually you'll find a carefully constructed tangle of sticks and twigs, a remarkable feat of bird engineering designed to provide security, stability, and comfort for the nest's fragile inhabitants—at least until they are old enough to fly away. Mother birds seem to instinctively know that their first priority is to build a strong nest, or their young chicks will never reach maturity.

Makes good sense, doesn't it? Many human parents fail to realize that children rarely grow strong in unstable, poorly constructed families. If your goal as a parent is to help your offspring eventually leave the nest as a young adult, then you'll want to make sure the nest is a strong one. It should be able to provide support that will enable your kids to develop fully, and it should provide an environment where they can develop the skills they'll need to build a strong nest of their own.

There's no denying that the vast majority of teenagers who have serious problems during their adolescent years are those who come from unstable families. Teens who are most vulnerable to substance abuse, premature sexual activity, delinquent behavior, and other kinds of social, emotional, or behavioral dysfunction are those who also have experienced more than their fair share of family dysfunction.

How do you build a strong nest? It doesn't happen as a result of chance or good luck. Parents who have strong family values intentionally create stable families. Planning is required. There is wisdom in the expression, "All things are created twice." There is first a mental creation, then there is a physical or second creation. You must first conceptualize what is to be created, then you do the actual creating.

Before a contractor can build a house, for example, he must first visualize what it will look like and then create a set of blueprints that describe it in great detail. With a good set of plans, there is an excellent chance he'll build the house he wants.

Another example is the book you now hold in your hands. Before it was written, an outline was created. I decided on the overall theme, the chapters that would be included, and what each chapter would cover. That was my first creation. The second creation was the writing.

Your family is no less important. If you want a strong nest, then you will want to decide what it will look like. You might start by asking yourself, "When my children are grown, how will they remember our family or describe it to others? What principles and ideals will they identify as being central to our family life?" Questions like these will help you to set a course for your family—to identify the core values that you want to instill in your kids.

A Family Mission Statement

Once you have identified the important principles that will govern your family, it's a good idea to write them down. Some families actually write family mission statements, to remind everyone in the family of their true identity and purpose. A written mission statement isn't mandatory, of course, but in today's world—with so much fuzzy thinking and so many outside influences—it's a good idea to have some kind of family constitution that reinforces your values and gives them additional authority.

Just as organizations and businesses have mission statements that clarify their purposes and goals, so your family can benefit from a mission statement that holds every member of the family accountable. It can provide a clear expression of your family's identity and can become the criterion by which you make important decisions and judgments. It can give continuity and unity to your family as well as direction, and it can be the changeless standard that gives your family its foundation.

"Isn't that what the Bible is for?" you may ask. Yes, absolutely. Your family mission statement should be able to identify the important biblical principles that you want to govern your family life. If you can articulate them clearly and apply them to your specific family, you will not only make them clear, but you will be constantly reminded to live accordingly.

You may not think writing a family mission statement is important, but keep in mind that if you don't create one for your family, your kids are likely to create one for you. One reason why many kids start believing that *they* are in charge of the family is because they don't see any leadership from their parents. Your kids need to know that their family is not drifting along aimlessly, but has some timeless underpinnings that can be identified and written down.

This is not something that you can write overnight. It will take some thought and may require several rewrites. You will want to review it periodically and make minor changes (or amendments) as time brings additional insights or changing circumstances.

The process can be just as important as the finished product. You might want to call a family meeting and allow everyone to provide input and feedback. While parents are the ones who must decide ultimately what goes into the family mission statement, including family members in the process can be a good strategy for encouraging good communication within the family.

Once your mission statement is written, treat it as a document of importance by having it printed or written in calligraphy and display it somewhere in the home for everyone to see. Don't just file it away.

The family mission statement examples in this chapter can give you some ideas, but you will want to compose your own. If you use somebody else's mission statement, you will never feel deeply about it or feel any obligation to live by it. If you will take the time to create your own, writing it from the heart, you and your children are more apt to follow it.

The writing of a mission statement for your family may seem a little strange or unnecessary. After all, your parents probably didn't write a family mission statement *(and you turned out okay!)*. But in today's world, children are understandably confused. Every day, they get hundreds of competing messages from the media and from peers about families and values; we can't assume that outside influences know instinctively what makes your family tick. Even if you don't have a family mission statement hanging on the wall, you definitely do need some way to communicate clearly to your kids what your family is all about. There should be no doubt in your kids' minds about what is important to you and what is expected of them.

In the Old Testament, parents are charged with teaching their children the commandments of God: "Impress them on your children. Talk about them when you sit at home and when you walk along the road, when you lie down and when you get up . . . Write them on the doorframes of your houses and on your gates"(Deuteronomy 6:7–9). While the Old Testament probably didn't have family mission statements in mind, it certainly did have in mind being clear and consistent about communicating the truth to children.

You can't expect your kids to know what they need to know unless you tell them and then reinforce what you tell them with your actions. If you want to give your kids a solid foundation for personal growth, give them a strong family identity that provides sound values and clear direction for their lives. That's a nest that is strong indeed.

THE TOM JOHNSON FAMILY

Our mission is to love and serve God, to be obedient to Him, and to make a positive difference in the world. We will love God by loving each other and honoring each other in word and deed. We will encourage each other to be all that God created us to be. We will stick together through good times and bad and always be thankful for what God has given us. Each member of our family is an important part of it and will contribute to the family unselfishly. We will put God first, not money or possessions or prestige. We will worship God as a family every Sunday morning in church. We will pray daily around the dining room table and at other times when we want to seek God's direction and help.

THE JEFF and MARIE JONES FAMILY

Our home is Christ's home.
That means we will ask "What would Jesus do?" in every situation.
Our home is based on Scripture.
That means that children will honor and obey their parents, and parents will love, protect, teach, and inspire their children to become all that God created them to be.

THE DONALDSON FAMILY CREED

* We will live each day to the glory of God, with gratitude, discipline, purpose, and joy.

* We will strive to treat each other with love, respect, and humility.

* We will seek God's will at all times.

Put It in a Strong Tree

Unless the Lord builds the house, its builders labor in vain.
—Psalm 127:1

We were sound asleep on a rainy night when a loud crashing noise behind our house startled us out of bed. I grabbed a flashlight and charged outside to investigate. What I found on the edge of our property was a tall eucalyptus tree that had toppled over during the night due to rain-soaked soil, gusty winds, and a very shallow root system. As far as I could tell, no damage had been done to anything of value, so we all went back to bed. I lay awake wondering if my chain saw and I would be up to the task of turning that tree into firewood.

The next morning I took a closer look and found that some serious damage had indeed been done. A family of chicken hawks had been living in that tree. Their nest hit the ground hard, as did the infant hawks that were found scattered among the debris. Sadly, none of them survived the fall.

Maybe there's a lesson there for all of us. If we want our children to eventually leave the nest as fully grown, well-adjusted adults, *then we need to build that nest in a strong tree.*

The Strong Tree of Faith

There is no stronger tree than faith in God. Even in today's postmodern secular world, most people acknowledge this is true, even though they may deny it in actual practice. Few would dispute that faith has provided strength and stability for countless generations of families since the beginning of recorded history. "Unless the LORD builds the house, its builders labor in vain" (Psalm 127:1).

Like the wise man who built his house on the rock (Matthew 7:24–27), wise parents build their homes on the rock of faith. God not only created the family unit (Genesis 2:24; Mark 10:9), but He is also the One who blesses and sustains it (Deuteronomy 6:1–2; 12:5–7). This is a truth that has stood the test of time. Parents who care about raising a healthy family will put faith in God at the very center of their family life.

First Things First

There is hardly a clearer biblical instruction for parents than the one found in Deuteronomy 6:4–9.

> The LORD our God, the LORD is one. Love the LORD your God with all your heart and with all your soul and with all your strength. These commandments that I give you today are to be upon your hearts. Impress them on your children. Talk about them when you sit at home and when you walk along the road, when you lie down and when you get up. Tie them as symbols on your hands and bind them on your foreheads. Write them on the doorframes of your houses and on your gates.

It is significant that this scripture identifies the first commandment—the one about loving God—as the one that is to be impressed upon your children first of all. How do you teach something like that to your kids—more specifically to teenagers? As we all know, it can't be done with preaching and platitudes. The only effective way to impress your adolescent children to love God above everything else is to model that behavior for them.

I was privileged to grow up in a Christian home. My dad was a building contractor and my mother was a full-time mom. But more importantly, they were both unabashed lovers of God. Nothing was more important to them than being in church every Sunday (morning and evening) and any other day of the week the church had services, which was quite often as I recall. I have

all kinds of wonderful family memories, but without question the most enduring of these are memories of my parents praising God, singing hymns and gospel songs, or standing up in church with tears streaming down their faces as they shared what God was doing in their lives. I can't tell you what an impression that made on me. Reading the Bible, praying together, and talking about spiritual things was so natural and normal in our house that I couldn't imagine families living any other way. My parents weren't perfect—we all knew that—but I never doubted the authenticity of their faith in God and their complete devotion to Christ. They not only talked about it; they lived it. It was their example that laid down the tracks for my own life.

There really is no better way to teach your children to put God first in their lives. If you yourself are doing all you can to stay close to God, your kids will be much more likely to want to do the same. You can't force your kids to become Christians. You have no control over what they choose to believe or not to believe. But you do have control over you—and what you do may become the pattern that your kids will follow.

Setting a Good Example

I have a good friend whose name is Dan. Like me, he's an avid fisherman. Unlike me, he has a really nice fishing boat and takes every opportunity to get out on the water. Sometimes I go fishing with him. He excitedly called me on a recent Saturday afternoon to tell me that the albacore tuna were biting offshore. "I'm going out after them tomorrow morning," he said. "Wanna go?"

You bet I did. But there was one problem. "Tomorrow is Sunday," I reminded him. "What about church?"

"Man, we can go to church any Sunday, but the albacore are only going to be around for a few days," he said. "We can get tapes of the pastor's sermon."

It was a point well taken, but still I had to turn him down. I can't remember a Sunday in my whole life when my father wasn't in church—and he was a busy man with a successful business. He'd often have to work late into the night to get things done, but he never missed church. He also had hobbies and loved to go camping and fishing. But never on Sunday. That was a lesson I learned well, and I have tried to teach it to my own kids.

"Dan," I said, "I hope you catch a lot of fish. But I also hope you understand that you might be sending your daughter a message you may not want to send—namely, that fishing is more important to you than worshiping God. I know that's not true, but kids don't always know that. Tell me, what are you going to say to her when she wants to go to the beach with her friends next Sunday instead of going to church?"

I hope I'm not sounding too self-righteous here. There have certainly been times when I've had to miss church for one reason or another (and not all those reasons were very noble).

But I want to make this point. The only way a parent can ever hope to teach a child to love God with all her heart and soul and mind is for that truth to emerge from what the parent has in his or her own heart and soul and mind. Only then can the lessons that come up at the table, at bedtime, on walks, in the busyness of the day, or the first thing in the morning have any credibility at all. Only when parents inwardly and outwardly love God and put Him first in their lives will children get the message that God is sovereign and worthy of our love and obedience.

Celebrate Your
Marriage Big-Time

Children need to know that marriage partners are more important to one another than the offspring of their marriage.

I f you are in a two-parent family, your wedding anniversary should be one of the most important holidays of the year. After all, without your marriage, there wouldn't be a family at all!

Marci and I have always made a big deal out of our wedding anniversary. We put it on the family calendar and start making plans weeks, if not months, ahead of time. Our kids always knew it was coming up. When they were children, we would sometimes do something special together as a family. One year we took them out of school for the day and went to Disneyland. We wanted them to understand how special our marriage (and our family) was. Celebrating with us somewhere they enjoyed communicated that very effectively. On other anniversaries, we left our children at home and went away for a romantic weekend trip—which also communicated volumes to our kids. They knew that we were away being romantic, having fun, and doing what lovers do. That can be a very reassuring thing for children, even if they can't imagine their parents doing anything like that.

More importantly, when couples make a big deal of their wedding anniversaries, it's often an indicator of the vitality of their marriage. It's unlikely that anyone would celebrate something that is unhealthy, dying, or already dead.

Love Your Spouse More Than Your Kids

The best gift you can give your kids is a strong and vital marriage. Children need to know that their parents' love for each other is greater than their love for their kids. That doesn't mean that parents love their children less—only that they love each other *more*. If you succeed at communicating that to your kids, they will also feel more loved. When children can see the love between their parents, they will know that there is plenty of love available for them.

There are many reasons why a strong marriage is important to your kids, but here are a few of the most important:

Strong marriages provide security for children. Teenagers especially need the security of a strong family. Adolescents experience a variety of internal developmental changes—physical, intellectual, emotional, and social—and the last thing they need in their lives is an unstable external environment. It's no wonder that the top worry of teenagers is the loss of a parent by death or divorce. Teens who live in homes where Mom and Dad are drifting apart often feel like they are losing their footing and are likely to seek solid ground elsewhere.

A strong marriage also provides children with a model from which they can learn to eventually relate to their own spouse. Many young people today are reluctant to get married, even postponing marriage for many years simply because they haven't observed a healthy marriage relationship between their own parents. And those who do get married often struggle in their marriages simply because they are forced to overcome the dysfunctional family experiences of their childhoods. It's hard to build a strong marriage when you don't really know what one looks like or how one works.

A strong marriage also makes it clear to your kids that you are in charge, that you are in control, and that you stand at the center of the family. This is very important. Kids who grow up believing that the family revolves around them are likely to be disobedient, disrespectful, and dysfunctional.

It may sound noble for parents to say that they put their children first, but in reality it's a prescription for trouble. Parents who put their children ahead of their marriage run the risk of raising extremely self-centered kids who are manipulative and demanding. If you make children the center of the family, you communicate to them that their needs are more important than anyone else's and that your role is simply to give them whatever they want, whenever they want it. This not only gives children an unrealistic view of the world, but it almost always turns parenting into a frustrating and unrewarding experience.

Healthy families are parent-centered families. In most cases, the marriage existed before the child (and produced it), and the marriage will exist after the child is gone. This is what makes it possible for kids someday to leave home and start families of their own. No one can be the center of the family and leave it at the same time. When children are at the center, they have no way to get out or grow up.

Of course, this does not mean that you should withhold love, nurture, and support from your kids, nor does it mean that you treat them like outsiders or neglect them in any way. The point is that you can't allow a child to rule the roost. You don't want to mislead him into believing that he is the most important person in the family and that his needs come before everyone else's.

A strong marriage provides balance in parenting. Moms and dads bring different roles to the parenting process. Boys and girls both benefit from having moms and dads who complement each other. Boys, for example, imitate their fathers and learn masculinity from them while they get their manners and nurturing from their moms. Mothers tend to "hang on to their baby" while dads rescue their sons by giving them the confidence they need to make it on their own. With girls, the roles are somewhat reversed. Dads are usually more protective of their daughters, while moms encourage independence and self-reliance. The balance is especially beneficial to kids during their adolescent years.

Protect and nurture the relationship you have with your husband or wife. Don't allow your career, your house, your kids, or anything else to destroy the love that you have for each other. Celebrate your anniversary! Make your children bring you gifts! Don't be afraid to leave your kids with sitters or with friends so that you can get away and be extravagantly romantic. If this sounds selfish, it isn't. On the contrary, it's giving your kids the best gift they could ever have—parents who love each other supremely.

Does this benefit your kids? You bet it does. Teenagers especially need to understand that Mom and Dad have something special going. They need to see you and your spouse touching each other, kissing each other, saying nice things to each other, and treating each other with love and respect. They need to know that there is nothing they can do to come between the two of you or to play one of you against the other. When your kids know this, they will not only be more likely to respect your authority, but they will have a solid foundation for their own views about love, marriage, fidelity, commitment, and the entire range of human values.

A Word of Encouragement to Single Parents

If you are a single parent, I'm sure that reading about the importance of a strong marriage might be uncomfortable or discouraging for you. But remember that it is addressed to couples only. Please don't take it as an indictment of you or of single parenting in general. While I have never been a single parent, I am well aware of how difficult it can be to parent alone. You face unique pressures and challenges that two-parent families are most often spared—but I am confident that God can provide you with what you need to be a successful parent.

This chapter is written to encourage couples to stay together and keep their marriages alive and well. But remember that the other forty-nine chapters apply to all parents, regardless of their marital status. Know that being single does not automatically disqualify you or anyone else from raising healthy, well-adjusted children.

Elect Yourself President-for-Life by Divine Right

Democracies may be fine for governments, but they don't work in families.

I'm glad I live in a free country that was founded on the principles of democracy, aren't you? But I am also glad that I grew up in a home that wasn't.

When I was a kid, my parents ruled the house like a king and queen. Their authority was absolute. They decided all the rules, and they enforced them rigidly and consistently. I never had the option of debating family policy or of electing a new parent who would be more to my liking. Our family was a monarchy that provided stability and security for me as a child and allowed me to have a relatively stress-free childhood. I never had to worry about where to go, what to do, or how to be. I just respected my parents and did what I was told—*or else*. Disobedience was never tolerated, and discipline was always swift and unambiguous—as it should be.

Democracies may be fine for governments, but they don't work in families. The last thing a child needs from his parents is a vote. What he needs instead is decisive leadership, authority, and discipline—and if you are the parent, it has to come from you.

In recent years there has been a growing trend away from authoritarian parenting to a more democratic style which encourages parents to listen patiently and nonjudgmentally to their children. Parents are encouraged to give them feedback in the form of opinions and guidelines and then allow them to make their own decisions. Today's parents are taught to reason with children, to appeal to their intellect, and to treat them as equals—giving them a voice in determining rules, chores, and privileges. All this is based on the widely accepted myth that too much authority can damage the fragile psyches of children and lead to their developing low self-esteem.

As noble and good-hearted as it may sound, the democratic family has never worked, and it's unlikely that it ever will. Parents who adopt a democratic style of family government usually end up with kids who lose respect for authority everywhere—not just in the home. More often than not, they come to believe that the world revolves around them, and that if you ignore, whine, argue, and manipulate enough, you can eventually have your way.

Parents As Dictators

The democratic family of today came into vogue as a reaction (or over-reaction) to the kind of authoritarian parenting which is most often caricatured by an unloving, controlling, meanspirited or abusive parent who sadistically demands unquestioning obedience of children at all times. Of course, parents who mistreat and abuse their children in the name of authority don't deserve to have children in their home at all. But the remedy for an abusive home is not the abdication of parental authority. Effective parents are authoritative, not authoritarian. They get respect from their children because they create rules that are good for them and enforce them firmly, consistently, and absolutely—with love and gentleness.

Author and psychologist John Rosemond recommends that parents adopt a style of parenting he labels a "benevolent dictatorship." You may be uncomfortable with that terminology because of the image we have of dictators like Adolf Hitler and Saddam Hussein. But *benevolent* dictators are different. They know how to balance love and respect (benevolence) with absolute authority (dictation).

In fact, the best model we have for our understanding of a benevolent dictatorship is the God of the Bible—who not only is our absolute authority but our loving heavenly Father. Just as God's law and God's grace coexist without conflict, so parental authority and parental love should do the same.

That kind of leadership is not tyranny at all. Parents who are benevolent dictators do not demand unquestioning obedience. They allow their children to express their opinions, and they listen to them with love and respect. But children must understand that they don't have a vote. The final decision always belongs to the parent. Benevolent dictators are not power-hungry control freaks who derive pleasure from bossing their kids around. Instead, they exert authority because they must. It's every parent's responsibility to govern effectively, and it's every child's right to be governed effectively. This will prepare children for the day when they must also govern their own families.

Unilateral versus Mutual Authority

As children grow older and become teenagers, they experience increased freedom and responsibility as the parents graciously hand it over to them, a little at a time. David Elkind, in his book *Ties That Stress*, differentiates between what he calls "unilateral authority" (where parents alone make the rules) and "mutual authority" (where parents and children share in the rule-making process). He observes that many of today's parents start out with mutual authority as their primary parenting style. Then, when their children become teenagers, those same parents try to exercise unilateral authority by setting limits and imposing rules, but their kids won't accept them. They inevitably rebel. That's because children can accept the transition from unilateral authority to mutual authority, but not vice versa. It's no wonder that some psychologists now advise parents that today's "new teenager" can't be expected to obey parents at all.

It doesn't have to be that way. Even while your kids are teenagers, you can make it clear that you have not relinquished the leadership role in your home. As long as your offspring are living at home, you remain the ultimate authority, even though you have graciously given them the right to make many decisions for themselves. *It's your home, not theirs.* Someday they will have a home of their own, and they will become the leaders in their own home. But until then—even though they may be fully grown—they have to live according to the rules. Your rules.

Incidentally, this will benefit both you and your teens when they get older. When it's time for them to leave, they'll probably be anxious to do so. Many teenagers today have no desire to leave home because they already have all the freedom they could ever want—and they don't see any reason to complicate things by taking on additional responsibility and expense by moving out. Why leave home when you can do what you want and have all the amenities of adulthood for free? You can't really blame kids for postponing their adulthood by mooching off their parents for as long as they can.

Don't Be a Geek

The decisions you make today about how you want to live your life will impact your home and your children in significant ways.

How to Be a Geek

1. Buy matching outfits for your family to wear to Disneyland.
2. Visit your son's first job and announce to all the other customers that you're his mother.
3. Forget the airline tickets after rushing your entire family to the airport.
4. Go to the mall with your teenager with curlers in your hair.
5. Go shopping with your teenager and have your credit card refused because you're over the limit.
6. Honk the horn when you pick your kids up at school.
7. Tell a joke to your kids' friends but forget the punch line.
8. Ride a bike to work.
9. Try to hold your teen's hand while crossing the street.
10. Take pictures of your daughter and her date before they leave home.
11. Rush up and hug your teenager when she wins the swim meet.
12. Offer to take your kids to the mall, but run out of gas on the way.
13. Start an ostrich farm in your backyard.
14. Turn all your son's underwear pink by washing them with your red sweatshirt.

The things we do that embarrass our kids. It's no wonder they want us to drop them off a block away from the school. Who wants to be seen with a geek!

When your children were little, they probably thought you were perfect, almost godlike. But around the time they became teenagers, somehow you fell off your pedestal and were banished to the land of the hopelessly uncool.

Don't despair. This has little to do with you. When kids reach adolescence, they have a compelling need to distance themselves from parents, even while they watch them more closely. This can cause teenagers to be very critical and condescending at times. You don't really have to do anything to deserve this; it just happens.

But parents often unwittingly distance themselves from their kids and exacerbate the problem even more by not taking care of themselves. They get out of shape, out of touch, and run out of gas. Just when they need all the energy and stamina and good humor they can muster, they let themselves get run down and their kids run off. It doesn't have to be that way.

How Not to Be a Geek

Don't worry, it has nothing to do with coolness. You don't have to be trendy or stylish. You don't have to keep up with all the latest fads and fashions. You don't have to act like a teenager or know the names of their favorite rock groups. Your kids don't want you trying to compete with them.

What they do need, however, is your personal well-being. They need you to stay healthy and happy. Pastor Myron Augsburger once put it this way: "You must first be a person, then a partner, then a parent, and last of all, a professional—whatever your profession might be: plumber, painter, politician, or preacher." In other words, you really need to take good care of yourself.

Some folks think putting yourself first is just being selfish. But I disagree. In fact, I've come to the conclusion that being happy is a moral obligation. We owe it to our spouses, our children, our fellow workers, our friends, indeed to everyone who comes into our lives, to be as happy as we can be. That's because if we aren't happy, then those who are close to us will also be unhappy. Nobody likes to be around an unhappy person. Miserable people just make everybody else miserable too.

The Significant Seven

There are no magic formulas for health and happiness, but here are seven things you can do to avoid being a geek:

1. *Stay close to God.* Spend time with Him. Practice the daily spiritual disciplines of prayer, Bible reading, and worship. You'll never be happy without nurturing your soul. As the psalmist put it, "Happy are the people whose God is the LORD!" (Psalm 144:15, KJV).

2. *Protect and nurture your marriage.* Love your spouse and keep your marriage full of passion and joy. Happy marriages inevitably result in happy couples.

3. *Make sure your work is satisfying and rewarding.* The best way to do this is to remember that your job (your occupation) is one of the ways you serve God. It doesn't matter what you do—whether you are a butcher, baker, or candlestick maker (or lawyer or software developer or grocery clerk). You can find meaning and purpose in what you do by remembering that "It is the Lord Christ you are serving" (Colossians 3:24). Your kids will benefit by having a parent who enjoys his or her work and comes home emotionally energized rather than completely spent.

4. *Find hobbies and recreational activities that you enjoy—and do them!* This will not only make you a more well-rounded person, but also it might offer some opportunities to share those activities with your family. One of my hobbies is music—specifically bluegrass music. As a family, we've gone to bluegrass festivals, attended concerts, had jam sessions in our home. It's no wonder that all three of my kids have become musicians themselves (although not *bluegrass* musicians!). It's good for kids to have fun with their parents and to know that their parents are capable of enjoying life as adults.

5. *Develop some enduring friendships.* It's unfortunate that so many adults (especially men) have such a difficult time finding and making friends. I am so grateful to a few close friends of mine who, over the years, have been such invaluable resources to me—as golfing or fishing buddies and as sounding boards and prayer partners. You not only need friends, but your kids need you to have friends. Your friends can serve as role models and mentors for your kids.

25

6. *Stay physically fit.* Exercise regularly, eat the right kind of foods, get medical checkups on a regular basis, avoid bad habits (you know what they are), and remember that your kids need you to be at your best.

7. *Become a lifelong learner.* Read books on a regular basis, take a class at a community college, go to seminary, attend a personal growth or business seminar, learn a new skill, develop a hidden talent, or volunteer to serve in a ministry or community program that gets you out of your comfort zone. Your life will be enriched as you explore new horizons, enlivening conversations around your house and helping your kids understand that education goes on forever.

Let these suggestions serve as reminders that life is short. Why not do all you can to make the most of it, to live it to its fullest? That really is God's will for you (John 10:10), and with His help you can do it. The decisions you make today about how you want to live your life will impact your home and your children in significant ways. It's no coincidence that healthy and happy kids generally have healthy and happy parents—and vice versa.

Don't be a geek. Take good care of yourself.

Act Your Age

Actions speak louder than words.

"No, Brandon, I'm not going to give you an advance on your allowance. Money doesn't grow on trees! Besides, it's wrong to go into debt so you can buy things you don't really need."

"Dad, didn't you just borrow $20,000 to buy that new Harley-Davidson?"

◆ ◆ ◆

"Jennifer, I really don't think you should wear such a skimpy bathing suit to the pool. It's just not decent."

"But Mom . . . my bathing suit covers more of me than yours does!"

◆ ◆ ◆

"Daniel, if I ever hear you using language like that again, you'll be on restriction for a month!"

"What's the big deal, Mom? Dad uses it all the time. Why don't you put HIM on restriction?"

◆ ◆ ◆

Ouch. Whether we like it or not, kids tend to follow our lead. If we want *them* to act their age, then (doggone it) we will have to act ours. It's a very simple truth that many parents fail to understand. Actions *do* speak louder than words. That is especially true when teenagers are doing the listening and watching.

If our goal is to get our kids safely into adulthood, then it only makes sense that we as parents model for them what it means to be an adult. Teenagers get very confused when parents fail to demonstrate such adult characteristics as responsibility, good judgment, and self-discipline. It's hard to teach kids to delay gratification or make wise choices when parents rarely do so themselves.

If you are prone to swearing in traffic, don't be surprised to hear some choice words from your teenager the next time they encounter a little stress. If you bend the truth on the telephone to get out of an unwanted engagement with a friend, don't be surprised when your son lies to you about his whereabouts last Saturday night. If you are a consumer of junk food, pornography, recreational drugs, alcohol, cigarettes, or are enslaved by addictive shopping or other bad habits . . . then don't bother to tell your kids that these vices are wrong or bad for them. "Do as I say, not as I do" is never very effective with teenagers.

If you don't believe me on this, try telling your teenager not to smoke while you light up a cigarette and blow smoke in his face. Or give her a lecture on the evils of alcohol while you swig down a bottle of beer. On second thought, don't try that. But you can imagine which message would come through the loudest if you did. What you say can't hold a candle to what you do.

The good news here is that you can have a huge positive impact on the lives of your kids by behaving in ways that reinforce what you want them to learn. Your basic beliefs and values, the true nature of your character, will be clearly communicated to your kids every day by the way you live.

If this sounds like a heavy burden to bear, keep in mind that no parent has the ability to be a perfect example. The only perfect parent is God. My wife once told me I was a model husband. I took that as a compliment until I looked up the definition of the word *model* in the dictionary. It's "a small imitation of the real thing." Actually, that's not a bad way to describe what it means to be a model. Hopefully we can be a small imitation, a reflection, of what God created us to be. We aren't perfect, but we strive to live as obediently as we can.

None of us do the right thing all the time, but our kids can learn a great deal about themselves and about life just by observing how we handle mistakes and failures. If we lose control of our temper and say things that are hurtful and unkind, we can apologize and ask for forgiveness. If we make a bad choice or commit a sin, we can admit our wrongdoing before God and before our family members, allowing them to become part of the restoration and growth process. Quite often, kids are most encouraged and strengthened when they learn that their parents aren't perfect, and that Mom and Dad must work hard to close the gap between the knowledge of right and wrong and their behavior.

Some parents worry that their past misdeeds disqualify them from being good examples or positive role models for their children. Again, our kids can learn much from their parents' life experiences—even bad ones. While it is generally not advisable nor helpful for parents to air dirty laundry in front of their kids, there are times when it is best to be honest and to let kids know that failure is part of life too. Everyone can learn and grow from the mistakes they make, but it requires honesty and a commitment to change.

Ultimately, teenagers learn about adulthood by watching the adults they have the most access to—their parents. When parents act selfishly, irresponsibly, or dishonestly, kids learn that this is normal adult behavior, and they most certainly will imitate it. Few children are mature enough to learn in reverse, that is, to become responsible by observing irresponsible parents.

Your kids may not listen to you very much, but you can bet they will be watching. You can help your teenager grow up by being grown-up yourself.

Invest Wisely

Your presence will always mean more than your presents.

It costs money to raise kids to adulthood—a *lot of money*.
A few years ago, I heard about a man who was something of a miser, extremely organized, very successful in business, and always careful about his investments and financial holdings. He was also the parent of twins—a son and a daughter.

For each of them, he kept a ledger—a thick, hardbound book with lines and columns printed in green ink in which he kept track of every penny spent on them. He wrote down the cost of diapers, baby food and formula, bottles, safety pins, school clothes, groceries, toothbrushes, and each tube of toothpaste. He tabulated their share of laundry detergent and toilet paper, their portion of electricity, water, and garbage collection, every pair of shoes they'd ever worn, Christmas gifts, allowances, even travel expenses figured at thirty-five cents per mile.

Year after year the man diligently kept his records. When his two children finally graduated from college, he presented each of them with their completed ledgers and two separate bills—each of them showing a total amount due of:

$1,456,365.21

Sound far-fetched? Actually, it's not. There are some parents who treat their kids from the time they are born as if they are less important than the money it takes to raise them. Or they worry so much about money that they make all their parenting decisions based on what's best for their bottom line instead of what's best for their kids.

If we're honest, most of us have probably stored up a few mental records of how much extra water one of our kids used during a shower, how much wasted food they left on their plate, or how much heat they let out the front door by not closing it. There's nothing wrong with being concerned about waste or with teaching children to be fiscally responsible. But when financial concerns prevent us from making good parenting decisions, or when they become a source of excessive worry and conflict in the home, we run the risk of communicating to our kids that money is more important to us than they are.

Let's face it. Whether you are rich or poor, raising children to adulthood requires a considerable financial sacrifice. According to one recent government calculation, a typical child in a middle-income family requires a twenty-two-year investment of just under a million and a half dollars. Unless you are extremely well-off, it's likely that you'll have to postpone many of your personal financial goals until your kids are grown and able to support themselves. But isn't that what we all signed up for when we became parents? It costs money to raise kids, but it's money well spent. There really is no better investment than the future of your children. You can't do better on Wall Street.

The Good Life

I'm amazed when I meet parents who insist they deserve the good life. They want big houses, fancy cars, designer clothes, jewelry, club memberships, cosmetic surgery, exotic vacations, and substantial investment portfolios. At the same time they insist they don't have enough money to enroll their kids in a good school, to support their church's youth ministry, to send their kids to college, or to provide other positive experiences for them.

Not all families can afford every possible advantage for their kids, but affluence is not a prerequisite for negligence. You don't have to be rich to make money more important than your kids are. Sometimes sacrifices need to be made, and it's wrong when children are the ones who have to make them.

Occasionally in my weaker moments, I've wondered how much money I would have now if I hadn't spent so much on our children. There's no question I would be financially secure right now. But I know I'm a richer man by far because my family has given me such joy. Material possessions are nice—they don't talk back, pout, or argue with you! But they also don't smile at you, give hugs, hold your hand, or plant a kiss on your bald head.

You can't buy good kids like you might buy the so-called good life. But ask any parent. Raising healthy, happy children beats raising your net worth any old day.

The Investment of Time

You have something far more valuable than money to invest in your children—your time. The story is told of three little boys who were outside playing. One of them said, "My dad is famous. He knows a lot of important people." The second boy said, "Well, my dad is rich. He owns businesses all over the world." The third boy thought for a moment and said, "Well, my dad is *home*." Which of those boys do you think was most proud of his dad?

In every working parent's week, there are approximately 168 hours. He or she probably spends 40 hours at work. Allow another 15 for driving to and from work, overtime, and lunch. Set aside 56 hours per week for sleep. That leaves approximately 57 hours each week to spend elsewhere. How many of those hours are spent with the family?

I asked a group of teenagers how much time each week they spent with their parents, talking or doing things together other than watching TV or being driven to school. The average time they reported was about ten minutes.

You've probably heard someone say, "I've never met a man who, on his deathbed, wished he had spent more time at the office." Money and success are good things, but they aren't worth the time they rob from your family.

One father I know gave his son a coupon book for Christmas containing 365 coupons, each worth one hour of the father's time over the course of the following year. The boy could redeem those hours as he wished. It was the best present that boy could have ever received from his dad.

Many kids today grow up in empty homes or in day-care centers because both parents are working hard to earn the money they think they need to raise their children and to maintain the lifestyle they want. While there's nothing wrong with both moms and dads having meaningful work to do, there is something wrong with parents who give the best hours of their day to their careers or their bosses and have nothing left to give their children when they get home. Kids need their parents more than they need the things their parents can buy.

Your presence will always be more important than your presents.

Circle the Wagons

Surround your kids with as many quality adults as possible.

Rock music	Political leaders
Parents	Schoolteachers
Television	The Internet
Peer group	Church youth leaders
Grandparents	Drugpushers
Movie stars	Family friends
Neighbors	Uncles and aunts
The advertising industry	The Bible

Influences: They play a huge role in the lives of your kids, especially when they become teenagers. Adolescents are at that special time of life when they look at the world through eyes that are newly opened. On the brink of adulthood, they begin making decisions about what kind of person they want to be, what they want to believe, who they want to pattern their lives after. And they are likely to make those decisions based on the important influences in their lives—or those that are most successful at attracting their attention.

Scary, isn't it? Especially when so many of those influences appear to be dangerous, destructive, or downright evil.

Unfortunately, it's not easy to control or to limit these influences when your children become teens. When they were little, you probably kept pretty close tabs on where they were, who they were with, and what they were doing. But now, it's not so easy to monitor their whereabouts or to prevent them from being with people you don't know. Part of being a teenager is having a private life that parents don't know everything about. You can be assured that your kids have one.

Keeping Things in Perspective

While you can count on there being many influences, both good and bad, vying for the attention of your kids—remember this: *You, Mom or Dad, remain the most important influence in your son's or daughter's life all the way through his or her teen years.*

You will hear plenty of expert opinions to the contrary. There is a widely circulated, oft-believed myth that parents no longer influence their teenage children. This false information has led many parents to distance themselves from their kids, to stop being involved, to surrender their kids to the outside influences in their lives. This is a serious parenting mistake.

In study after study, researchers confirm that parents are impossible to unseat as the primary influence on their adolescent children. Parents invariably come out on top, followed by grandparents, teachers, coaches, religious leaders, and same-age peers. The media most often comes in dead last. No matter how glamorous they may be, rock stars can't hold a candle to the influence of Mom and Dad.

Certainly when kids reach adolescence, the influence of celebrities, teachers, friends, and the media increases as parents compete more vigorously for attention and allegiance. But parental influence still reigns supreme. Only when parents abdicate their rightful position of influence do lesser influences fill the void. This is what I call "influence by default."

Circling the Wagons

Excluding parents, the most important influence of teenagers are adults outside the home—teachers, coaches, youth workers, parents of friends, members of their extended family. That's why I believe you should do all you can to surround your kids with as many quality adults as possible. In other words, circle the wagons.

I remember watching those old westerns featuring caravans of rickety covered wagons heading across the prairie. They would inevitably come under attack and hastily form a tight circle as a defensive move. The circle provided protection for the women and children and gave the brave pioneers at least a fighting chance to hold off the enemy.

All fiction, no doubt. But the concept works to illustrate my point. The best protection you can give your kids against negative worldly influences is to circle the wagons—surround your kids with adults who care about your kids and will serve as role models for them.

I don't know about you, but when I was growing up, I stayed out of serious trouble simply because I had too many people to disappoint. I had grandparents, uncles and aunts, family friends, teachers, coaches, youth-group leaders, mentors of all kinds who really *cared* about me, and I knew it. Not only did I not want to disappoint them, I wanted to make them proud of me.

It's sad that so many kids today have no one like that in their lives. Sometimes not even their parents care what they do or what they become. It's no wonder they are so vulnerable to outside negative influences. They have no protection against them. There are no significant adults in their lives who care what they do—one way or the other.

When our daughter, Amber, was a youngster, my wife overheard a conversation she had with a friend. Her friend was bragging about her church—how large it was, how impressive the music was, and how many activities it provided for her family. We, on the other hand, attended a very small church at the time with none of those bragging points. I wondered what Amber would say. Did our small church embarrass her? After listening to her friend, Amber thought about it and replied quite matter-of-factly, "Well . . . the people in my church love me."

I'm so glad that my kids have had people in their lives who loved them while they were growing up. They never had the benefit of living in the same town with their grandparents and extended family as I did (although they see them frequently), but our church family became a support system of love and encouragement for them. They showed up at our kids' ball games, graduations, and birthday parties. They prayed for them when they were sick, and they helped discipline them when they did wrong. Kids need to connect with people outside the home in order to validate and strengthen what they get inside it.

Believe me, the absence of positive influences is a far greater danger to our children today than the presence of negative ones. When we talk about circling the wagons, we aren't suggesting that we shield our kids from bad people so much as we mean to expose them to as many good people as we can.

Anticipate Their Adolescence

It's a lot like what happens when a caterpillar is turned into a butterfly: the change can be pretty dramatic.

Jason used to love going out with us to the restaurant or to the movies. We had such nice family outings. But now he flatly refuses to be seen with us in public."

◆ ◆ ◆

"I miss the days when I could dress Dawn for school. She always looked so nice. But now she won't let me in her room. It takes her over an hour to get ready for school, and she goes off looking just awful."

◆ ◆ ◆

"I don't know how Chris got so lazy! We used to call him 'Daddy's little helper.' Now he hardly lifts a finger to help out around the house. He just sleeps and listens to music."

◆ ◆ ◆

"Melissa has changed; there's no question about it. She used to come home from school and tell me about her day. We used to talk about everything. Now she goes in her room and shuts the door. I feel like I'm losing her."

◆ ◆ ◆

"Devon was always the runt of his class. But this year he just started growing. We can hardly keep him in clothes anymore!"

◆ ◆ ◆

Change: That's what adolescence is all about—transformation and change.

And lest you think all those changes are bad, think again. In most cases, the changes that take place in children when they reach adolescence are normal and not always unpleasant—for kids or their parents. Some adjustments are necessary for everyone, of course, but adolescence is not an illness; it doesn't need a cure.

The purpose of adolescence is to turn children into adults. That's exactly how God planned it when He created the human race. He decided that it would be best to start us off as children and then—in just the right time frame—change us into adults. It's a lot like what happens when a caterpillar is turned into a butterfly; the change can be pretty dramatic.

God Himself experienced this change. Remember when Jesus became an adolescent? In the second chapter of the Gospel of Luke, we find Jesus at age twelve staying behind in Jerusalem to hang out with some teachers at the temple. He wasn't deliberately disobeying Mary and Joseph, but He obviously neglected to inform them of His plans. They traveled a day's journey before noticing His absence, which is probably the equivalent to driving five hundred miles on the freeway today. They were justifiably worried and probably a bit angry, but to their credit they kept their cool even though it took three days to find Him.

We don't know much about what happened next except that Jesus went home with His parents and was obedient to them (Luke 2:51). I'm glad we are given this brief picture of Jesus as a twelve-year-old. It's a classic example of the adolescent experience, which often catches today's parents as off guard as it did Joseph and Mary.

Like Jesus, our kids have a great desire to spread their wings and fly as they approach adulthood. They need room for exploration, for going on intellectual adventures and spiritual pilgrimages. And they don't usually ask permission for it. Wise parents prepare themselves for these changes and begin to make adjustments as their kids grow and develop. If you want to guarantee that you will have rebellious teenagers, all you have to do is not grow with them. Just keep thinking of them as toddlers or treat them like grade-school children. Parents who complain that their teenagers act like children are usually parents who treat them like children.

Don't be surprised by the conflict and discomfort that invariably occurs at adolescence. There are few living things that don't experience growing pains.

Growth and pain just seem to go together—like milk and cookies. In fact, the more rapid the growth, the greater the travail is likely to be. And in something as close and intimate as a family, the growing pains of one member are certain to become the pains of everybody. The challenge is to turn those pains into *panes*—windows of opportunity for better communication and understanding.

Are you ready to change when your kids do? Do you know what to expect when your kids begin their journey toward adulthood? To get ready for your child's adolescence, you don't need to become an expert on it, but you can learn enough to respond to your changing son or daughter in appropriate and positive ways.

Everybody Experiences It

Adolescence is one thing you have in common with your teenager. The best way to understand what your kids are experiencing at adolescence is to get in touch with your own. Do you remember? Most adults repress (or forget about) their adolescence, say psychologists, because it was not a happy experience. That's why it's often hard for adults to appreciate the perils of puberty. We just don't remember them.

Pull out your old junior-high or high-school yearbook. Take a trip back to your teen years. Try to remember how you felt trying to fit in with the right crowd at school or when your boyfriend or girlfriend broke up with you or when you were teased for saying something stupid or being too fat or too skinny or too short or too tall. You might even remember how unkind and unreasonable your parents seemed to you at that age.

The world your kids are growing up in has changed a lot since you were a teenager, but the adolescent experience has not. It is universal and time-less. You went through it and survived; chances are pretty good that your kids will too.

Adolescence Is a Process

While the invention of adolescence has helped us better understand how children develop and grow and has led to better schools and other programs for youth, it has also had some unfortunate consequences. For example, it now takes a whole lot longer for kids to become adults. In the past, children looked forward with great anticipation to becoming adults once they reached puberty. It wasn't long before they were regarded as "young people." But today, children look forward to becoming teenagers—not adults—and they remain thus for as long as possible. Some thirty-year-olds today identify more with teenagers than they do with adults their own age.

This is why I believe that it's important to understand adolescence not as a separate stage of life, but as a process which changes a child into an adult. Think of it this way: Before adolescence, your child is 100-percent child. Then, shortly after adolescence begins, they are 99-percent child and 1-percent adult. With each passing day, they become a little less child and a little more adult. Finally, when their development is complete, they are 100-percent adult. The time it took for the transition to take place is adolescence. That time can vary greatly from person to person, but in the past it rarely took more than three or four years. It shouldn't take as long as it does today.

Rather than thinking of your adolescent children as teenagers, try thinking of them more as young emerging adults—and treat them accordingly. This will encourage more adultlike, responsible behavior from them, and it will make their journey toward adulthood a lot less confusing and considerably smoother.

Get ready for your child's adolescence. But don't get ready for it like people in South Florida prepare for a hurricane. Instead, go to the library and study up on adolescence, find resources that outline what parenting a teenager involves, and observe teens in your church youth group. Preparing in advance will enable you to welcome your son's or daughter's adolescence by looking forward to it with understanding, anticipation, and joy. It's something you can celebrate together.

Anticipate Your Obsolescence

Parenting is a wonderful privilege and responsibility, but it wasn't meant to last forever.

It's not that I don't like my parents. I know they love me and that what they do they really think is in my best interests. It's just that I feel trapped. I know I'm young, that my judgment is not perfect, and that I'm going to make mistakes. But they make mistakes too! I'm not a little kid anymore. I have a brain, and I can figure things out for myself. I just can't stand them telling me what to do all the time. Sometimes I just wish my parents would let me move out and get an apartment of my own. I could manage; I know I could. They'd be surprised. I really don't need them anymore."

Like it or not, there comes a time in every young person's life when they would like to make their parents disappear. And that time usually comes sooner than we anticipate. In fact, the process begins at early adolescence.

Your kids need you around more than they realize, of course, but in a different way. No longer do they want you supervising their every move. They don't want Mom telling the barber or hair stylist how to cut their hair. They don't want Dad telling them where they can go, whom they can be with, or what they can do with their money. No longer do they want someone else running their lives.

So when your kids become teenagers, they may try to fire you as their parent. But don't worry, they'll hire you back as a consultant. As your kids change, so does your role in their lives.

This shouldn't come as any surprise. Parenting is a wonderful privilege and responsibility, but it wasn't meant to last forever. Remember, the goal of parenting is to work yourself out of a job. Your purpose is to provide care for children until such time when they can take care of themselves. It's a temporary job with planned obsolescence built right into it.

This is hard for some parents to accept, especially if their identity or self-worth is wrapped up in being a mom or dad. Stay-at-home moms are especially vulnerable to feelings of loss when children get older. In today's world there's a lot of pressure on women to seek fulfilling careers outside the home. When a woman chooses to be a full-time mom, she generally does so with the conviction that full-time motherhood *is* a career choice. It's a job requiring specific skills and responsibilities that include the supervision and care of children. When the children no longer need or want that constant supervision and care, it's like finding yourself unemployed.

Feelings of irrelevance are heightened when this coincides with Mom and Dad's midlife years—when they find themselves struggling with other disagreeable career and identity issues. The inevitable loss of one's youth and the realization that options are getting more and more limited can create some unsettling feelings of anxiety and frustration.

These are natural life changes that happen to just about everybody. Time marches on, and the changes that come with it are inevitable. The best way to cope with them is to anticipate them, welcome them, and adjust to them accordingly.

Many parents tend to resist any changes in their parenting role. But kids change whether parents do or not. When parents don't make adjustments to the changing developmental needs of their kids, they risk alienating them and inhibiting their growth. To be willing to change is to communicate respect and love.

Stages of Parenting

Below are five parenting stages that represent changes in your child's development as well as corresponding changes in your role as a parent.

These can help you evaluate your readiness for the day when you will set your young adult free. They don't necessarily correspond to particular ages (which varies from child to child), but they do represent a progression toward independence and self-reliance that we want to facilitate and encourage rather than to inhibit.

1. Catering

Child: I'm hungry!

Parent: Here you are, sweetie, some delicious mashed carrots. Yum yum.

During the first year or so of your children's lives, your role is primarily that of caretaker or servant. You set your schedule according to theirs and jump every time they cry, whine, or make a demand on you. You are at their beck and call, allowing them to interrupt conversations and indulging them in all sorts of behavior that would not be tolerated in older children. You

44

treat them like royalty and wheel them through shopping centers and other public places in portable thrones while passersby stop to pay homage.

It doesn't take long for infants and toddlers to conclude that the world revolves around them and that everyone else exists to do their bidding. After all, they have known nothing else.

2. Controlling

Child: I'm hungry!

Parent: Then eat your green beans! No dessert until you do!

As your children reach their second birthdays, they experience a revolution that overturns their previous understanding of reality. This revolution leads to a *revelation* that they are not the center of the universe after all—*you are*. You are no longer their caretaker or servant, but their authority figure and teacher. When they were in diapers, you paid inordinate amounts of attention to them. But now that they are older (and for the foreseeable future), they are required to pay attention to you. No longer do they make the rules; you do.

Understandably, this turn of events can come as a real shocker to toddlers who preferred things the way they were. They don't usually surrender easily. They often throw tantrums, hurl themselves to the ground, scream bloody murder, fling plates of food to the floor, and otherwise make their parents believe they are savages. That's why this age is often called "the terrible two's."

Still, it's important for parents to make this transition as early as possible and to stay the course. If you don't settle authority issues early and completely when children are young, you leave yourself wide open for some tough sledding when they become teenagers.

3. Coaching

Child: I'm hungry!

Parent: Don't eat a lot of junk before dinner, Jason. You'll ruin your appetite.

Once children are clear on the issue of authority, you can start playing the role of coach. This usually occurs when your kids are still in their preteens.

It involves giving them some power and control over their lives while you still have absolute authority. While they may get to make some decisions on their own, you continue to set the rules. You impose the limits, you determine where the boundaries will be, and you provide healthy doses of coaching, teaching, reprimanding, and correction. Kids are allowed more freedom at this stage.

4. Consulting
Child: I'm hungry!
Parent: If I were you, Jason, I'd eat some fruit. The apples in the refrigerator are delicious.

When kids reach their midteens, they resist controlling and even coaching (which they usually interpret as nagging), and they object to any attempt to micromanage their lives. Like a quarterback on a football team, they now want to call their own plays and live with the consequences. They want coaching and counsel only when it is asked for. They will eventually seek it, but it can't be forced on them.

5. Caring
Child: I'm hungry.
Parent: Lord, please help Jason find a job.

This is the last stage of parenting that releases the child into adulthood. At this stage, you care about your kids and want them to make good decisions, but basically they are on their own. You are finished parenting. No longer should you interfere with their lives in any way except by invitation. Your adult children should know that you are always there for them, willing to offer counsel or help when it's required and asked for, but they are now in total control. As a parent, you influence them only with your love, support, and prayers.

No clear line of demarcation separates these stages in the parenting process. They blend together in varying degrees all during your parenting years. For example, you may find yourself being a *controller* when it comes to the use of the family car, but you may serve as a *counselor* when it comes to helping your teen decide which courses to take in school. You may *coach* her regarding the purchase of a prom dress while limiting yourself to *caring* about her date selection. In other words, the process varies with age, maturity, and specific issues.

The important thing to remember is that you are crucial to this process. Don't underestimate your role. While you may be approaching obsolescence in parenting, you are never unimportant. What you do matters, and your influence is decisive. The key is learning to shift from control to influence.

When children become teenagers, they start resembling the adults they will eventually become. They are off the launching pad, so to speak, moving quickly toward independence. The initial indicators may not be exactly what you had envisioned, and you may wish to reverse the process somehow and force your teenager to remain a child—but you can't. It's too late. It's time to start letting go, to work with your child to function independently someday. This understanding is crucial to your survival as the parent of a teenager.

Don't Buy All
the Bad News

There are millions of teenagers all over the world who are doing their best to live decent and responsible lives.

Janine used to be so sweet. When she was little, she would give me these cute little cards with hearts and happy faces on them. They would say, 'I love you, Mommy,' and nice things like that. I would read her stories every night, and she would sit and listen to every word. We would take long walks together and get ice-cream sundaes. I just don't understand what happened. She changed overnight. She doesn't want me around. She abuses me. She's turned into a monster."

"Brian and I always had a good relationship. We were very close. When he got home from school, he couldn't wait to tell me about his day, and he always wanted to show me his school papers. He was so proud of them. Sometimes he would sit in my lap. He wasn't embarrassed about it, and we would just talk. It was really very wonderful. But then he changed. Now when I walk into the room, he gets up and leaves. He doesn't seem to care about school anymore. I think he may be using drugs. He shaved his head and looks like a freak. I don't know what's going on in his life because he won't tell me. I feel like I've lost him."

Scary, isn't it? It's common today to believe that this is the norm—that all children go bad when they become teenagers and that there's not much anyone can do to prevent it. We hear, "Just wait. No matter how pleasant and sweet and innocent your child might be as a youngster, as soon as that first hormonal surge of puberty occurs, your beautiful child will turn into an uncontrollable monster who will wreak havoc on your home and your personal life for a decade or more."

That summarizes what has come to be known as the Myth of the Teenage Werewolf, and it strikes terror into the hearts of parents who believe it. Further, it makes good parenting almost impossible because it basically means that parents are powerless to do anything more than accept the inevitable. I spoke with one newly married couple who glumly insisted that they were not going to have children at all—simply because they didn't want any teenagers in their home.

Parents aren't the only ones who fall for the myth. When I travel, I sometimes like to give people a simple word association test. What comes to mind when you hear the word *teenager*? What I often hear in response:

School violence

Sex, drugs, rock-'n'-roll

Gangs

Irresponsible

Materialistic

Suicide

Scary looking

Delinquency

Curiously enough, I then ask those same people to tell me about a teenager they know personally, and they often describe a kid who in fact is none of the above. They tell me instead about a youngster they know who sounds like he or she should be nominated for sainthood.

That's because the Myth of the Teenager Werewolf is, of course, only a myth—a ridiculous stereotype that is grossly unfair and unrepresentative of the vast majority of kids. That's not to say that adolescence doesn't produce uncomfortable changes and challenges for everyone. Of course it does—it always has.

Tongue-in-cheek warnings about the perils of parenting teenagers have been around for a long time, but the modern idea that all adolescent children are inevitably transformed into frightening and uncontrollable presences in the home did not capture the public imagination until recently.

What has led to this negative perception of adolescence in recent years? It can be partially traced to cultural phenomenon such as the drug epidemic of the sixties and seventies, the image of rebellious teens in film and on television, and the general breakdown of authority in society. Also factor in the violence and moral depravity found in today's rock music lyrics, the alarming rise in youthful violence, teen pregnancies, and suicides that we hear about in the news so often. But while these negative stories are certainly a cause for great concern, it's important to keep in mind that the actual number of kids who make headlines are a very small percentage of the total age group.

Over the last few years, we have heard story after story about murderous teens in small towns like Pearl, West Paducah, Jonesboro, Edinboro, Springfield, and Littleton. We have heard little about the millions of teenagers all over the country who are doing their best to live decent and responsible lives.

Case in point: The same week in 1999 when two high-school boys in Littleton, Colorado, murdered a dozen of their classmates, 73,000 Christian teenagers gathered in the Pontiac (Michigan) Silverdome. They were there to sign a pledge abstaining from sex, illegal drugs, and alcohol, and "to live with honor, to accept responsibility for [their] behavior and to respect authority." Did you hear anything about that? I didn't think so.

It would be wrong to ignore the fact that there are many struggling teenagers in today's world, and it would be wrong to discount the gravity of the problems they face. But it is also wrong to accept the notion of today's out-of-control "new teenager" that paints all kids with the same unfriendly brush. If we don't refute this misconception, our kids will spend their entire adolescence trying to prove that it's not true. Many others will succumb to the generalization and live down to everyone's expectations. I heard one teenage girl admit that she had sex with a willing partner "just to get it over with." After all, that's what everyone expected of her.

The importance of believing in your kids, having high hopes for them, and encouraging them to become all that God created them to be cannot be overemphasized. If you expect your children to be rebellious and troublesome during their teen years, they will probably do their best to live up (or down, as it were) to that expectation. Don't let the Myth rob you of the relationship that God ordained for you and your teenager.

Focus on the Four Rs

Parents must model qualities of character, or children will never learn them.

And you thought there were only three!
No, we're not adding another R to readin', 'ritin' and 'rithmetic. There are four *other* Rs that are actually more important than those well-known core curricula of academics. The Four Rs represent the core competencies of life—the basic foundation upon which a person's success and happiness as an adult rests. They are:

RESPECT

RESPONSIBILITY

RESOURCEFULNESS

REVERENCE

The Four Rs are not as easy to teach as the Three Rs. They aren't easily defined, and they can't be taught in a classroom. Some schools and churches have tried, but they really have to be taught at home. Unless parents model these qualities of character in front of their children and give them opportunities to learn them from experience, they won't be learned at all. In fact, the Four Rs are what this entire book is about. They are values that are naturally instilled in children who grow up in a home that is "Four-R Friendly."

Respect

Respect is obviously in short supply these days. Kids of the past may have been expected to show respect for their elders and for those in authority—but not today. Postmodern youth are taught to respect themselves, not their elders or anyone else—and to question authority, not to accept it or obey it. Unfortunately, the "Don't trust anyone over thirty" mantra of the sixties has come back to haunt parents who rebelled against authority when they were teenagers.

Growing up in a world of disrespect has had serious consequences not only for parents but also for kids. Children naturally look up to older people for guidance and direction. When it is not found, they naturally experience anxiety and confusion.

Additionally, when young people lack respect for particular adults in their lives, they end up lacking respect for adulthood in general. It's no wonder so many youth today are so ambiguous about the prospects of becoming an adult. Who wants to become something or someone you have no respect for?

Respect is something our kids need to learn for their own benefit. When kids learn to respect others, they also learn to respect themselves. You must give respect before you can get any, even from yourself. And self-respect plays a huge role in how young people mature. Kids with self-respect do better in school, have better friends, make smarter choices, and generally live happier and more successful lives than those without it.

So how do you teach kids to be respectful? Certainly not by demanding, begging, or pleading. Respect has to be earned. Parents earn respect by establishing their authority early in the lives of their children and then being competent and consistent year in and year out. Children need and want parents who act like they know what they are doing. You don't have to *actually* know what you are doing, but you have to *act* like you do. Confident parents instill confidence in their children, which anchors their sense of security. When kids feel secure, they respect the source of their security.

Of course, respect is a two-way street. Especially with teenagers, parents need to *show* respect as well as *expect* it. Kids who are treated respectfully are more likely to be respectful. Mutual respect doesn't mean that parents and children have equal amounts of authority in the home. Instead, kids respect their parents by obeying them. And parents respect their kids by expecting them to obey. This kind of mutual respect results in greater trust and more freedom for both parents and kids.

Responsibility

Once upon a time, children learned to be responsible by having lots of it. Parents of the past often had large families not necessarily because they loved children but because they *needed* them. My grandparents lived on a farm and raised ten children. When each child was old enough or strong enough, they were given responsibility for gathering eggs, milking cows, plowing fields, or harvesting crops.

But in today's world, kids have an easier childhood but a harder time learning responsibility. They aren't expected to contribute to the economy or to the welfare of the family, so they just assume that someone else will take care of everything for them.

To become a capable adult, your teenager will need to learn responsibility both for himself and for things outside of himself. Responsible people are reliable, trustworthy, accountable, faithful, and dependable. They carry through on projects and finish what they start. Responsibility includes being competent and capable, and it involves a willingness to delay instant gratification for a greater payoff at some point in the future. No one is born this way. It is something that every person must learn, and the best place to learn it is at home.

One way we teach responsibility in the home is by assigning chores. When children are small, they can begin by taking responsibility for picking up their toys or clearing their own plates from the table. As they grow older, they can contribute more to the family by sweeping, dusting, running a vacuum cleaner, taking out garbage, washing cars, feeding pets, doing laundry, or caring for lawns and gardens.

Resourcefulness

A resourceful person is a creative person. In this context, the word *creative* doesn't describe artistic talent, but it refers to the ability to solve problems. A resourceful person looks at every problem as a challenge—another opportunity to explore, experiment, adapt, or invent. A resourceful person is a flexible thinker, one who can look at things from a variety of angles and use both trial and error and persistence to find solutions. Rather than giving up, resourceful people find a way to win.

You can make your kid a winner by teaching him resourcefulness. Allow him to do more things for himself, build his tolerance for frustration by not indulging him, and limit the number of toys and entertainment options he has access to. Television's greatest threat to your kids is not in the amount of sex and violence it portrays but the time that it robs from them to play and be creative. Young children between the ages of two and five and young adolescents between the ages of eleven and fourteen have tremendous capacities for exploration, discovery, and imaginative play. When these kids spend hours sitting in front of a TV, they are unlikely to engage their creative or problem-solving skills. Resourcefulness is something that has to be encouraged, practiced, and developed. It doesn't just come from good genes.

Reverence

Reverence is more than being good in church. Reverence is a sense of wonder and awe that flows from gratitude for life and for the Source of it. It is getting goose bumps from hearing great music, seeing the majesty of nature, gazing at stars ablaze in the night sky, smelling a rose, or experiencing the mystery of a birth. It is a sense of wonder that compels us to worship.

Reverence is an appreciation of the sacred and the holy in all of life. Reverence has inspired almost everything worthwhile that humanity has ever achieved—in art, music, literature, health, education, science, and civilization itself. Reverence provides people with a sense of significance and motivates them to accomplish great and beautiful things.

Sadly, many young people growing up in today's aggressively secular postmodern world have no real understanding of this and find themselves handicapped as a result. They lack purpose in life because they live only for themselves. They lack confidence because they feel alone. They lack motivation to live decently because they have no authority. They lack hope because they have no sense of the eternal.

Teach your kids reverence for the things of God. It is the spark that gives respect, responsibility, and resourcefulness their power.

Give Them
the Rite Stuff

The vast majority of youth drift through adolescence without knowing where they stand.

Once upon a time, Half-boy was born, a boy with only the right half of his body. As you might expect, he felt unhappy and incomplete. During his childhood he was loved. But as he grew older, he became a source of constant irritation, embarrassment, and confusion for his family and the entire village. Nevertheless, Half-boy continued to grow, at least the part of him that could be seen.

Finally his half-ness and incompleteness grew unbearable to him. His pain grew more evident to everyone around him. One day he left the village, not knowing where the path might lead him. He stumbled along until he reached a frightening and mysterious place where the path crossed a wild river. At that crossroads, he encountered another youth much like himself, who had only a left half of his body. Cautiously, the two half-boys approached each other and suddenly began to fight and roll in the dirt. They tumbled into the river and nearly drowned. But finally, after a great struggle, they emerged from the river not as two boys, but as one.

Dazed and disoriented, the new whole-boy began walking back to the village, feeling very unsure of himself. He didn't want to return to the place of his youth, but he could not stop himself. On his arrival, an old man greeted him. "Welcome home!" he announced. "You are back in the village where you were born. And now that you are whole, the dancing and the celebration can begin!"

And everyone in the village did join the celebration, especially the Half-boy who had become whole.

◆ ◆ ◆

This myth from the lost culture of Borneo illustrates the significance of ancient rites of passages that were once common to celebrate a child's transition into adulthood and the acknowledgment by the family and community of that adulthood.

In 1 Corinthians, the apostle Paul wrote, "When I was a child, I talked like a child, I thought like a child, I reasoned like a child. When I became a man, I put childish ways behind me" (13:11). When did Paul become a man? How old was he? Today, we might assume eighteen or twenty-one. But Paul, who undoubtedly had his bar mitzvah like other Jewish boys at age thirteen, assumed his manhood at that time. The bar mitzvah (or bat mitzvah for girls) is still practiced by Jewish communities to commemorate a child's transition to adulthood. The ancient ceremony and the celebration afterward provide a memorable, tangible way for the family and the community not only to recognize a youth's newly acquired status as an adult but also to confer on him new privileges and responsibilities.

A bar mitzvah is a rite of passage—something that has more or less been discarded on the junk heap of history. The term *rite of passage* is only used metaphorically today, usually to describe a first in someone's life, like a first date or a first taste of lobster.

But years ago in less industrialized (and perhaps more *civilized*) cultures, rites of passage were commonly used as a way to help young people know exactly where they stood in relationship to the world around them. Children looked forward to the day when they would leave their childhood behind and be given the rights, respect, and privileges of adulthood.

Period Parties and Other Rites

Rites of passage for children were usually connected with puberty, the onset of adolescence. For example, a *Kinaalda* is an ancient ceremony still practiced among some traditional Navajo and other native-American tribes celebrating the first period (menarche) of their daughters. On the occasion of the initial menstrual cycle—an obvious physical marker of a girl's transition to womanhood—the tribe gathers to honor and celebrate the young woman's new birth. Rather than a girl's first period being an embarrassing inconvenience, a nonevent as it is for many today, it was something to anticipate.

I remember when my daughter reached puberty. My wife discreetly informed me that Amber "got it" (her period), and I realized then that things would never be the same for her. We didn't throw a party, of course, but with a bouquet of flowers and a hug, I let her know that I knew and that I understood the significance of this day in her life. She had become a young lady, a young woman. No longer was she a child, and no longer was I going to treat her that way.

There are few rites of passage for young people today. Most children never know when they become adults. Recently the Sweet Sixteen party has made something of a comeback among middle-class families, some of them costing thousands of dollars. Its purpose is to celebrate a girl's maturity, her "coming out." There are still *quinceaneras* in Hispanic communities and *debutante balls* for the very affluent. Organizations like Outward Bound offer "vision quests" for boys—solo wilderness experiences designed to develop courage and character in young men as they move forward into adulthood.

Some churches still conduct *confirmation* as a rite of passage, a way to initiate a child into church membership or full participation in the sacraments. In some Mennonite churches, young adolescents are provided with adult mentors on their twelfth birthday in a ceremony that takes place before the entire congregation. This commemorates their passage into the adult community.

But the vast majority of youth drift through adolescence without knowing where they stand. They may look forward to the day when they get a driver's license or graduate from high school, but even those milestones often go unnoticed and unacknowledged as significant events in their lives. Many youth desecrate their own graduation ceremonies with disorderly or lewd behavior simply because they don't attribute much meaning to them.

But youth desire rites of passage, nonetheless. Some create pseudorites of passage to prove to themselves and to others that they aren't children anymore. For example, some youngsters join street gangs and willingly participate in initiation activities like drive-by shootings and other violent crimes. Such activities really aren't all that different from ancient rites. An Eskimo boy killing his own seal or an African boy killing a lion was a demonstration of reaching manhood. Other kids engage in sex, become pregnant, smoke cigarettes, or use drugs—all as ways to express their emerging adulthood. They do these things simply to announce to the world around them, "We aren't children anymore."

Adultified Children

What has made this even more confusing for many kids today is the blurred line between what is considered age-appropriate activities and behaviors for children and adults. In the past, children dressed like children, and adults dressed like adults. I can remember having to wear Buster Brown shoes and dungarees with suspenders to school. But today, preschoolers are likely to wear the same designer labels and expensive shoes their parents wear. When I was a child, we looked forward to high school to play football or to participate in other team sports with uniforms, strenuous practice sessions, and coaches who would yell at us and make us competitive. Today children as young as six participate in highly competitive team sports which have become more work for them than play. Children of the past were protected from adult information not suitable for young eyes, ears, and minds. Today children are exposed to every imaginable form of human depravity at younger and younger ages.

Professor David Elkind uses the term *vanishing markers* to describe the erosion of these signposts along life's way that give young people a sense of where they stand. The loss of markers in modern society has resulted in what he calls the *adultified child*—a gradual blending and blurring of the line between childhood and adulthood creating additional stress and confusion for youth who are in the process of identity formation.

New Rites

As parents, we can provide rites of passage for our kids as they grow and reach milestones in their lives. These new rites don't have to be elaborate or expensive celebrations, but they can be significant events that communicate to young people that they are getting somewhere, that they are growing up.

When I was a youngster, I often worked for my father, a general building contractor. He taught me to drive nails, use a Skilsaw, and frame houses. I'll never forget the day he gave me a special gift—a deluxe leather nail apron which I still have. It was just like the ones worn on the job by other carpenters who worked for my dad. It was his way of saying to me, "You are now officially one of my men." That message was not lost on me, and from that day forward I accepted that role with pride.

A mom and dad shared with me a humorous incident with their eleven-year-old daughter. They were in the car one day when mom noticed a foul odor coming from the backseat. She turned to the daughter and said, "Janine, I think it's time for you to start using deodorant." Janine grinned and shrieked, "Yayyyyy!" Much to the parents' surprise, body odor was a simple rite of passage for their daughter.

I don't recommend buying a can of Right Guard to celebrate your child's emerging adulthood, but there are many ordinary events in family life that can be transformed into rites of passage. A birthday celebration or a promotion from one grade to another can become an occasion to truly celebrate your child's growth and maturity. Events such as these become significant when they are acknowledged and appreciated as such, especially by parents. A few examples:

* Getting a checking account
* Being allowed to sing in the church choir
* Participating in the men's (or women's) ministry at church
* Having a weekly breakfast meeting with Mom or Dad
* Getting your bedroom redecorated (new "adult" furniture)
* Starting to shave
* Going on an extended hunting or fishing trip with Dad
* Being allowed to wear makeup
* Getting a driver's license
* Getting a job
* Teaching a Sunday-school class
* Traveling by air without adult supervision
* Getting expensive perfume as a gift from your dad
* Buying a suit
* Being allowed to stay home without a baby-sitter

* Going to a ladies' tea with Mom
* Ordering from the adult menu at a restaurant
* Being given new responsibilities at home
* Getting a car to drive
* Going on a mission trip abroad with the youth group

These are only examples. Some parents are going further and creating unique rites of passage which communicate clearly to their children what it means to be an adult—articulating their new rights and responsibilities as young men and women. For example, in *Raising a Modern-Day Knight*, pastor Robert Lewis proposes to Christian parents an elaborate rite of passage for boys. The idea is based on a model from medieval knighthood—incorporating a family crest, a wilderness experience, a ring, and a variety of ceremonies at puberty, high-school graduation, college graduation, and marriage.

All of our kids need to know that they are growing up, and even more importantly, they need signals from us that we know. We may not be able to restore ancient rites of passage for them, but certainly we need to be there with them to celebrate the events in their life that move them closer and closer to adulthood.

Influence Their Influencers

To teenagers the three most important things in life are (1) my friends, (2) my friends, (3) my friends

No doubt about it. In the minds of most teenagers, friends easily outrank parents in terms of their redeeming social value, their knowledge of *truly important things*, their trustworthiness, their ability to give unconditional love and acceptance, and of course their overall coolness. Little children need playmates, but teenagers need friends. That's a sure sign they are growing up and becoming an adult.

But don't forget: Friends are of great importance to your kids, but parents are more important and more influential. Your kids will not admit this until they become adults and have children of their own—but it's true. Friends exert enormous influence in matters of the moment—the music they listen to, the clothes they wear, what they do for fun, how they look—but parents lay the tracks for ultimate issues like values, character, and faith.

Are there exceptions? Of course. Sometimes the short-lived influence of friends can have long-term consequences. We all know of young people whose friendship choices led to drug addiction, sexually transmitted diseases, or prison terms. I have grieved with parents over the loss of their children in needless auto accidents involving groups of teenagers under the influence of alcohol. Parental influence may be a powerful force in the lives of teens, but it is not always able to prevent bad decisions with disastrous outcomes. Every relationship involves a certain amount of risk.

We shouldn't fear the friendships our kids develop. Friends serve an important function in the lives of kids trying to determine who they are apart from the family. When they were little, they felt secure knowing they were loved by their parents. But as they grow up, they need acceptance outside the home. They know that they won't live at home forever, so they need to test their ability to have meaningful social relationships. This is all a part of growing up, and it shouldn't be discouraged or disallowed.

It would be nice if you could handpick your kid's friends for them, but that's not possible. All you as a parent can do is to provide your children with the best environment possible so that good friendship choices are available to them, and then pay attention to the friends your kids choose. That's why I use the phrase "influencing their influencers." You play a significant role in the relationships your kids choose outside the home.

Move to Mayberry

Ever think your kids would be better off living in a place like Mayberry? Never mind that it only exists on late-night reruns; you probably wouldn't want to live there anyway. Sin and fallen human nature are everywhere. Even seemingly idyllic places like Mayberry are going to have their share of crime, drugs, abusive families, and bad influences. There really are no perfect places to raise children.

Environment does make a difference. Some communities are a little safer, a little more conducive to raising healthy families than others. The relative decency of a community can be difficult to assess, I realize. But if you have the luxury of being able to choose where you live, select a place where family values are strong and where your kids have the best shot at finding healthy relationships outside the home.

Your Mayberry may be less a town than it is a good school or good church. If your kids go to a private Christian school, for example, they'll be more likely to find Christian friends. There is no guarantee that kids who attend private Christian schools will be good influences on your kids, but the odds are better. If you can choose between public, private, or charter schools in your area, visit them and check them out thoroughly.

Join a church with strong family programs—one that cares about youth and provides ways for them to be involved in ministry and discipleship. There is a greater likelihood that they will find friends there who believe as they do and who will support them in their walk with Christ. Peer pressure works both ways; it can be positive as well as negative. When teenagers have friends who are willing to stand firm in their faith, they usually do likewise.

Birds of a Feather

Kids, like adults, choose friends who are a lot like themselves. For that reason, one way you can *influence their influencers* is by giving your kids such a high view of themselves that they will be less likely to choose friends who will drag them down.

Every teenager experiments to some degree with friendship choices. I can remember as a youngster trying to make friends with some of the school hoodlums just to see what it would feel like to have them as my friends. I imagined myself strutting around school with those guys, looking tough, carrying a switchblade knife, beating people up, no longer being picked on by the bigger kids. Of course, none of this ever came to pass. Those tough guys didn't want me as a friend, and I knew it. I ended up having friends who were pretty much like me.

That's how relationships work for most kids. They want to fit in, so they look for a group where they will feel most comfortable, where other kids share their interests, backgrounds, and values.

That's why the best protection you can give your kids against poor friendship choices is to give them a self-image that won't fit in with the wrong crowd. Ultimately, young people develop their sense of who they are from their parents. Kids who have grown up in an atmosphere of neglect, abuse, or constant criticism come to believe they can't do anything right, that they are good for nothing, that they won't amount to anything. That compels them to seek out relationships with other *losers*. If your kids suffer from low self-esteem, they'll find comfort hanging out with others with low self-esteem.

How do you help your kids develop a positive view of themselves? Self-esteem has to be earned. Kids who learn to make their own decisions, take on responsibility, make positive contributions to their families or their world—

these are the kids who have self-respect. They are also treated respectfully by parents and others, which boosts their confidence and self-esteem.

Friend-Friendly Parents

Do you know the names of your kids' friends? Do you know anything about their families? If you want to influence your kids' influencers, get to know your kids' friends.

That doesn't mean you should intrude on your teens' friendships. Most teenagers get pretty annoyed when parents get nosy about their friends, try to act hip around them, or even talk to them. *"I can't stand it when my dad starts asking my friends questions when they come over. Like he's trying to be friendly. I can't help it; it drives me crazy."*

So how can parents be friendly toward their kids' friends?

First, avoid criticizing them or prejudging them. Sometimes kids fear bringing their friends around because they know their parents will give them the third degree on their background, their opinions, and their personal lives. If you communicate that you trust their choice of friends, they'll be more apt to bring them home, to introduce them to you, and to give you a chance to get to know them.

Second, let your kids know they can invite their friends for dinner, stay overnight, or participate in a fun family activity. Doing so will also encourage your kids to choose friends who are more compatible with the whole family.

Third, make your home a place where kids feel comfortable hanging out. Stock the refrigerator with sodas and the pantry with snack food. (If there is food, they will come!) Don't worry about the spills, the wear and tear on the carpet, or the kind of music being played on your expensive new stereo system. Don't worry about getting your flowers trampled while the kids are playing hoops in the driveway. At our house, we put in a swimming pool, tied a giant rope swing from the eucalyptus tree in the backyard, built a tree fort, put in a basketball hoop, and did everything we could to make our home a kid-friendly place.

Remember that while your kids probably don't want you encroaching on their friendships, it's possible for you to become a mentor to one or more of your kids' friends. This more often happens by accident than by design, but it happens. There are many young people who later credit the parent of a friend as being a significant adult influence in their lives. You really can influence your kids' influencers.

Let Go and Let Them Grow

Kids who are greatly inconvenienced by their own mistakes usually learn what they need to learn.

Here's a quick quiz for you.

At what age do you think your teenager should be allowed to make his or her own decisions, without parental interference, regarding these issues?

_____ Their choice of friends

_____ Their curfew

_____ The music they listen to

_____ How to spend their money

_____ What movies they see

_____ What classes they take in school

_____ Whether to attend church or not

_____ Whom they date

_____ Getting their homework done

_____ How their bedroom is decorated

Sorry, no answers are provided at the back of the book. But hopefully you aren't completely stumped. Every parent needs to decide at some point when to begin letting go of their kids—giving them some control over their lives. You can't wait until your kids are completely grown to start releasing them into adulthood.

When your children become adolescents, they need less control from you and more opportunities for them to rehearse their adulthood. That doesn't mean you withdraw completely from their lives, but it does mean that you start giving up control in favor of coaching and consulting. Your teenager needs guidance, direction, and limits from you as well as your permission to grow up. That means allowing them to live their lives with as little parental interference as possible. *Some* interference will be necessary, of course, but it should decrease with time until they are finally ready to leave home.

If you wait too long to give your kids the freedom they need, not only will you make it more difficult for them to achieve independence and self-reliance, but you may also end up causing the very things you want to prevent. Young people who aren't allowed to grow up while they are teenagers usually have to play catch-up for the rest of their lives. Parents who resist letting go of their kids when they are young adolescents have greater difficulty letting go when they have reached mature adulthood.

Parents As Micromanagers

In the business world, micromanagers are sometimes called "control freaks." They hover over their employees, making sure they don't make mistakes. They may give employees some responsibility, but they never allow them the freedom to do things on their own. This type of management style breeds job dissatisfaction on the part of employees, as well as a lot of resentment and anger. The irony of it all is that employees who are micromanaged usually end up doing worse, not better. Micromanagement in the workplace invariably results in more communication problems, more conflict, more dishonesty (as employees try to cover up their mistakes), and more disloyalty (as they seek the first opportunity to leave and find a better job).

In the same way, parents who micromanage their teenagers usually get the same bad results. Teenagers, unlike employees, can't resign and go find somewhere else to live, so they either rebel or just give up trying to be responsible and successful on their own. Ironically, this only causes parents to be more controlling, which causes kids to be even more rebellious and irresponsible, and the cycle continues.

How is this cycle broken? By remembering that the best way to hold on to your kids while they are teenagers is to let go.

Don't be a parental micromanager. You want to empower your kids through the orderly transfer of control and responsibility over their lives. This isn't done all at once, but little by little. Certainly balance and finesse are required, for if you withhold freedom and responsibility too long, your kids may rebel. But if you give too much freedom too soon, they may abuse it and make the kind of serious mistakes from which recovery is all but impossible. Nobody said parenting was a breeze.

The Old Rope Trick

If you give kids too much rope, they're liable to hang themselves with it. Although that may be true, it doesn't justify keeping kids on a short leash all the way through their teen years. Granted, we love our kids and don't want them to make mistakes they will regret later on—but it's not always in their best interests to try preventing these mistakes.

Quite frankly, it's usually not love that inspires our urge to protect, but our need to control. We like things done correctly, and we don't want to be inconvenienced by children who do things incorrectly. So we try micromanaging their lives to make sure they don't get into any serious trouble.

Everybody learns best by making mistakes. It makes sense, therefore, that when we prevent our kids from making mistakes, we also prevent them from learning. Teenagers need enough rope to make the mistakes they need to make in order to learn from them. In other words, it's not bad for them to hang themselves once in a while. They will learn, as we all did (and still do).

Teenagers are not stupid. If you are clear on the rules, limits, and consequences, go ahead and give them a chance to fail. This is called *trust*. If this sounds too risky to you, remember that you still have an important role to play in all this. You set limits; you coach; you consult. Unfortunately, some parents blow it on this point. Permissive parents are often so uninvolved that they fail (or won't take the time) to make sure their kids learn what they need to learn. When mistakes *are* made (and you can count on them), your job is to help your teenager understand what happened, why it happened, and how to keep it from happening again. There's no need to nag and lecture. Mistakes can be their own teachers by making sure consequences are applied and enforced. You don't need to get angry and upset when your kids mess up. Let *them* get angry and upset instead. Kids who are greatly inconvenienced by their own mistakes usually learn what they need to learn.

Remember, it's better for your kids to make mistakes now while you're around than for them to make them later when you're not. Give your kids some rope and remember: longer rope—less tension.

Keep Your Distance
but Keep Close

"Mom, I can't believe you! You're not being fair! I hate you! Why can't you just get out of my life?!"

Most teenagers at some point develop a severe case of parent allergy. Their parents repulse them. Your mere presence in the room can make their skin crawl. They will try to get away from you, to distance themselves from you. If you try to sit down with them and have a conversation, they will squirm, take deep breaths, tap their feet, and roll their eyes. They will act like you aren't there or that your time has expired and you are now infringing on theirs. All this is normal teenage behavior.

Lest you lose too much sleep over this situation, remember it's not about you. You didn't cause this. To teenagers, parents represent childhood, and it is childhood, not you, that they are trying to distance themselves from. They want to discard everything associated with their childhood, and parents are just one of those things. That's why they sometimes wish you would disappear.

You won't, of course, so they just make you feel like a pariah. This can be quite disheartening if you aren't expecting it. Nobody likes rejection, but it's almost inevitable for parents of teenagers. When kids are pulling away and pursuing their independence, it can feel like you are losing them completely.

Staying Close While Staying Away

It's possible to stay close to your kids even while they are pulling away. Keeping close and keeping connected aren't opposites but two sides of the same coin. Closeness just has to be redefined. Children show closeness by sitting next to you on the sofa and giving you hugs and kisses. Teenagers show closeness by allowing you to meet one of their friends or letting you drive them to the mall. Sometimes they show closeness by not leaving the room when you walk in. You have to take what you can get.

You can't stop your teenager from becoming more independent. Autonomy is a developmental necessity for adolescents. The trick is to find new ways to stay connected, to communicate, to be together. Your son or daughter probably won't jump up in your lap, wrap their arms around your neck, and fall asleep in your arms like they once did, but that doesn't mean you can't still be close.

Interestingly enough, teenagers want closeness too. Even while they are asserting their independence and avoiding parents at every turn, down deep they want a good relationship with Mom and Dad. But their parent allergy sometimes makes it impossible.

So if they can't make you disappear, they usually disappear themselves. They may go into their room, close the door, and turn on the stereo, only to come out about four years later. As much as they might like closeness, they don't know what to do or how to do it. Old ways of relating to Mom and Dad just don't work anymore. So they either vanish or act like you are invisible.

That's why we need to take the initiative to find new ways to stay connected with our kids. They aren't likely to do it themselves. They don't know how. It's easier for them to just keep their distance.

Respect Their Need to Not Be You

The first step toward staying close is to let your teenager know that it's okay for them to separate. Give them the distance they need. This may mean knocking on her bedroom door before entering or not forcing him to go with you to visit Uncle Henry and Aunt Gladys for the weekend. You may even need to rethink your next family vacation to give him time to be with friends.

When our kids were teenagers, we rented a condominium at the beach only twenty-five miles from our house just so our kids could invite their friends to join us for part of the time. This allowed us plenty of time to be together as a family, but it also allowed them time to be with their friends and not with us. Actually a vacation like that is a lot easier than trying to figure out how to keep your kids entertained twenty-four hours a day. We have some great memories of those vacations at the beach.

Find Some Common Ground

A dad recently asked me if I thought it would be a good idea for him to buy an old broken-down 1956 Chevy sedan that his fifteen-year-old son found for sale in the paper. The boy wanted his dad to help him rebuild the engine and restore the car to its original condition.

73

I asked the man if his son really wanted to do that. His answer was yes. I asked him if he knew how to restore cars. Again, yes. I asked him if there was room in their garage to work on the car. Yes. I asked if he had the time and the money necessary to complete such a project. Yes.

I told the man to run—don't walk—to the nearest telephone and make an offer on that car. Most parents would kill for the chance to have something like this project fall into their lap. Do it!

When I discovered that my kids loved to fish (like I do), I went boat shopping. I bought a small, all-purpose boat that not only could be used for fishing but also for water skiing, knee boarding, tubing, and other watersports. Yes, I know boats are expensive (a hole in the water into which you throw lots of money), but I have to tell you that the money we have thrown into that hole has been one of our best investments. We have spent literally hundreds of hours with our kids on that boat. (We still enjoy it now that the kids are grown.)

A few years ago I noticed my son Corey out behind the house hammering away at a woodworking project. He was trying to build a skateboard ramp out of some old pieces of plywood and scrap lumber, enjoying the construction of it more than anything else. That prompted me to ask if he would like to help me build a toolshed out in our backyard. I drew up plans for what would eventually become the Taj Mahal of toolsheds, complete with a gable roof, windows, and skylights. Our lawn mower and garden tools now live in luxury. The project took a couple of months to complete, but Corey and I had a great time working on it together. He also learned a few things about construction.

The key here is to find some common ground. What can you and your kids do together that you both enjoy?

Some parents and teens share a love of sports, either as participants or as fans of a favorite team. Some enjoy playing golf, working out at a gym, or running. I heard of one dad who traveled with his son by train to five different cities, attending major league baseball games in five different ballparks. The time on the road together, traveling by train, sleeping in hotels, and enjoying baseball was a true male-bonding experience for them. Other parents have found that their kids enjoy such things as camping, backpacking in the wilderness, rock climbing, surfing, scuba diving, music, martial arts, computers, photography, painting, shopping, sewing, cooking, flying model (or real) airplanes, even skydiving. The possibilities are endless.

Put Them on Your Calendar

You can also stay connected by scheduling time with your kids on a regular basis.

When Nathan was a seventh-grader, I invited him to go out to breakfast with me once a week. Being a growing boy, he didn't mind getting up early in the morning for food. Early every Wednesday morning, we dragged ourselves out of bed and went to a local restaurant where we had a hearty breakfast and a little conversation. I didn't use that time to lecture or scold. I listened and found out what was going on in his world and shared with him a little of what was going on in mine. Surprisingly, we kept this up for six years—until he graduated from high school. Once we got into the habit, despite his parent allergy, our Wednesday-morning breakfasts became a special time for us.

You may not need to schedule breakfast with your kids, but you probably need to make sure that you are getting enough time with them to interact in a positive, adult-to-adult way. Some parents do it every night before bedtime or driving their kids to or from school. Some parents schedule "dates" with their kids, going to sports events, movies, or out to dinner. In today's busy world, there is a strong likelihood that unless you become more intentional about scheduling some time with your kids, you won't get any.

Stay an Adult

You don't have to become a teenager to connect with your kids. Some parents mistakenly believe that the best way to stay close to their adolescent children is to immerse themselves in youth culture—to learn the names of all the rock groups and teen celebrities, the current lingo, the trends, and fads.

You don't have to do that, and quite frankly, your kids don't want you to. That's why they are into all that stuff in the first place—because you aren't. It's doubtful that you could keep up with it all anyway, as most kids change their preferences weekly.

On the other hand, don't completely ignore what your kids are into. If they get the idea that you don't care about their world, they may get the idea that you don't care about them. Listen and learn what you can out of respect and try to understand their need to be different from you.

If you stay connected to your kids during their teen years, you will not only be in a better position to guide them and influence them along the way, but you will build a foundation for the relationship you will have with your kids for the rest of their lives. Do you want to be friends with your adult children? The best way to insure that you will is to stay close while they are still in your home.

Prompt Their Passions

Parents should help their teens discover and develop not only what they are good at but also what brings them the most joy.

Several months ago, I was invited to speak at a junior-high youth retreat. Upon arriving I was greeted by a thirteen-year-old named Brian. Within a minute or two, he asked me if I had a title or theme for the talk I was going to give. I thought that was an interesting question coming from a junior higher, so I asked him why he wanted to know. He said he had a laptop computer and was in charge of making PowerPoint presentations for the youth group. He was going to put my talk on PowerPoint.

Since I knew nothing at all about PowerPoint or how to use it, I was both intrigued and impressed. I gave him a theme for my talk, and he disappeared. An hour or so later, Brian found me again with his computer and showed me a colorful graphic design for my talk, with my name appearing magically in the center, then disappearing again with a swoosh. Now I was even more impressed. Eventually he had my entire outline—with every point and sub-point—zooming in and out of the presentation which was projected onto a big screen while I spoke.

Helping Kids Discover Their Passion

It was pretty obvious to me that Brian, Boy Wonder of PowerPoint, had discovered his passion. He had found his niche. PowerPoint was something that he not only knew how to do, but he loved doing it. He was excited about it, and it gave him an opportunity to use his gifts and talents in a unique and very rewarding ministry.

Every kid needs to discover their passion—their niche—and be encouraged to pursue it. It could be drawing cartoons, building model airplanes, reading books, collecting seashells, or raising llamas. To parents, such things may seem foolish or a complete waste of time and money. Yet these activities may offer clues about the kind of work in the young person's future.

When our son Nathan was a teenager, I wondered if there would ever be any redeeming value to his obsession for collecting, gluing, and painting miniature models of Star Wars characters and other strange creatures from science fiction and mythology. Today he is a youth pastor—and lo and behold, he supplements his rather skimpy youth-pastor income by meticulously painting tiny miniatures of strange creatures for a Hollywood filmmaker who uses them for special effects. He did not inherit his patience for this kind of work from me.

It's not easy to predict what a kid's passion in life will be. As parents, we often have big dreams for our kids—but they may not be the dreams our kids have for themselves. We may want them to excel academically or in athletics, or we may want them to follow in our footsteps, perhaps to take over the family business.

Think back a moment. Can you honestly say that you are doing now what your parents wanted you to do when you were a teenager? My father wanted me to become an architect. He was a building contractor, and his dream was that someday I would design the buildings that he would build. We would be a team. I learned the building trades and excelled in my drafting classes in high school. There was nothing wrong with this dream, and I'm glad that I learned all that I did. But when I was in college, architecture didn't inspire me the way youth ministry did. Sometimes God has different dreams for our kids than we do.

I know a man who really had his heart set on his son playing baseball. As a frustrated athlete himself, he imagined his son hitting home runs and throwing runners out at the plate. But the youngster never showed any real interest in sports. Instead, he wanted to play the violin. To the dad's credit, he didn't argue but found a good teacher and encouraged his son to play. Today this young man lives in Nashville and is one of the most sought-after session musicians in country music.

One of the biggest struggles of adolescence is learning to be comfortable with who you are and how God made you. Teens waste a great deal of energy trying to be what they are not. They have so many people telling them what they should be or who they should be like. Parents, teachers, friends, the church, the media—all offer competing messages about what's best, what's cool, or what's God's will. All of this can be confusing for kids who need to just be themselves and find their own way—which they must do for their own happiness and fulfillment.

Bringing Out the Best in Your Kids

Here are a few ways you can help prompt the passion in your kids:

1. *Affirm their uniqueness.* Your family is made up of unique individuals, each with different talents, personalities, abilities, and gifts. If you have ever taken a personality test (such as the Myers-Briggs personality profile), you know how complex a person's personality can be. Some are very introverted while others are very outgoing. Some are detail minded; others see the big picture. Some are creative; others are analytical. Some are thinkers; others are doers. None of these traits are better than others—they are just different, and they result in different kinds of people. When you require an introvert to act like an extrovert, it's like asking a right-handed person to write left-handed. It can be done, but it's difficult, and the results aren't very good. In the same way, we need to realize that each young person is unique, and one of our jobs as parents is to help him discover what he does best.

2. *Avoid comparisons.* It's easy to compare kids to their siblings, to other people's kids, to their friends, to other "good kids" we know (or have heard about), or even to ourselves. We don't like it because our son or daughter isn't taller, thinner, smarter, more polite, less clumsy, or a better Christian. Even if you don't say anything, kids will pick up signals of disapproval or disappointment from you. Learn to love and appreciate your son or daughter for who he or she is right now.

3. *Put their interests ahead of your own.* In other words, let go of your need to look good in front of your friends. (They won't think any less of you if you don't have perfect kids.) Stop trying to live your life through your kids. (It's okay if your teen isn't popular or athletic like you always wanted to be but never were.) Don't worry if your teen doesn't choose that high-paying career track. (Trust that it's better for your child to be happy than to be rich.)

4. *Expose them to possibilities for passion.* Don't be so overprotective of your kids that they miss out on chances to have new experiences that might ignite their passion and open new possibilities. Let them explore their world and see what's out there that might interest them or excite them. We all know people whose lives were changed almost instantaneously by being exposed to someone or something that inspired or motivated them to pursue their passion. A prime example of a person who followed his dream is an airline pilot who as a youngster was invited to visit the cockpit of an airplane. There is a successful lawyer today who visited a courtroom during an eighth-grade field trip and a prominent surgeon who years before admired the doctors who treated her while she was hospitalized.

5. *Nudge a little.* If you notice your son or daughter doing something well, encourage them to pursue it further. A mother shared with me how she noticed her high schooler giving careful instructions to a group of children about how to play a game. She did such a good job of explaining the rules and making things clear to the children that the mother told her later, "You know, honey, you would make a wonderful school-teacher. You really handled those children so well." The daughter later pursued a career in childhood education.

Kids are often so busy chasing what others want them to be that they don't notice for themselves what they are good at. As parents, we can be observant and encourage our kids to follow their natural bent in life, the way God created them to go. Sometimes all it takes is a nudge, a little prompting. Proverbs 22:6 says to "Train a child in the way he should go." The word *train* in that verse is used in the same way gardeners train a tree limb or sapling. The idea is to train a child along their natural bent so that they will become beautiful and productive.

If your teenager shows an aptitude for computers, make sure he has access to one. If she has talent as an actress, let her join a drama club or take acting lessons. If he enjoys taking things apart and putting them back together again, tour a junkyard and find some cool stuff to dismantle. And don't worry if your son changes his mind several times before he settles on a hobby or interest that really suits him.

Our goal is to help kids discover and develop not only what they are good at but also what brings them the most joy. Too many adults are in occupations that they don't like. If your son or daughter can find a niche, their God-given passion, and then follow it to their eventual vocation, they'll find the best way to achieve happiness and fulfillment in their life's work. And the best way will be their way.

Don't Let School Get in the Way of Their Education

When I was his age, I loved high school. I got good grades. I was on the student council, the cross-country team, the French club . . . but Jason hates school. He cuts classes. He won't do his homework. I just don't know what's the matter with that kid.

Most teenagers aren't too fond of school. They may enjoy being with their friends at school, and they may like particular classes, teachers, or activities. But it's hard to find kids who think of school as anything more than a giant inconvenience with little relevance to their lives. Some kids actually think of school as a kind of prison for teenagers, a place where they must serve sentences imposed on them by parents and society. And now with so many schools requiring students to pass through metal detectors and armed security guards, they may not be far off the mark.

Most schools, both public and private, are doing the best they can to provide good education. Some resemble the schools we attended—with just as much school spirit and just as many dedicated teachers and administrators as those we remember. Not all schools are as bad as we hear, and quite a few are much better than we think.

While some kids actually like school, gaining a good deal of satisfaction from excelling and scoring high grades, most just try to make the best of it. Report cards continue to be a perennial hot-button issue between parents and teenagers, mainly because parents see grades as the first true predictor of their offspring's future. If they aren't getting good grades, parents panic. We imagine them not getting into a good college . . . not getting a good job . . . not being able to support themselves . . . not becoming a productive member of society.

The Job of School

Unless kids have some appreciation for the important role that school plays in their lives, they will probably underachieve as students. That's why they need to understand that school is their job, their primary occupation, while they are still at home.

School performance is not just about getting good grades. While it's important to become competent in those academic subjects that make up a high-school education, equally important is the role that school plays in building character. The discipline that school requires is a steppingstone toward emancipation. If a young person can succeed in school, then he or she will not only be better equipped to succeed in a career but also in life. School provides youth with the means to develop and practice such essential emotional and behavioral skills as responsibility, autonomy, perseverance, time management, initiative, self-reliance, and resourcefulness. Those are the skills and qualities of character that are necessary for a person to become a fully functioning adult.

Impress upon your kids that regardless of what they plan to someday become—they are, for now, first and foremost a *student*. They don't necessarily need straight As, but they do need to organize their lives around the goal of getting an education. If they can succeed as students, they have laid a good foundation for succeeding at whatever else they decide to do.

Not All Schools Are the Same

Because school is so important in the lives of teenagers, parents should do all they can to provide the best educational opportunity possible. That doesn't necessarily mean an expensive private school, but you should examine your options carefully. Many parents never take the time to consider the many educational choices that are available. Despite what most people think, all public schools are not the same. If you have the option of relocating your family to an area where better schools are provided in the public-school system, you should seriously consider doing so. You do have choices.

What about private schools? Or more specifically, what about *Christian* schools? Unfortunately, not everyone can consider this option because of the expenses involved and the lack of good Christian secondary schools. But if a good school is available, and if you can afford it—I recommend it. My wife and I have spent a small fortune sending our three kids to private schools, but we have no regrets whatsoever. There is no better investment than a good education for your children.

But be careful. Don't put your kids in a private school just because you can, or because you fear the public-school system. Private schools should be chosen strictly on the basis of location, academic standards, quality of the faculty, number of graduates who move on to good colleges, extracurricular activities, theological or philosophical underpinnings, and moral and ethical standards. Do plenty of research on any school that you are considering for your children. Talk to the teachers; interview students; spend a day on campus visiting classes; get a feel for the campus life. This is the only way to make an informed decision about whether the school is a good fit for your kids or not.

Some parents enroll their kids in private Christian schools simply to keep them away from worldly influences like the teaching of evolution, classmates who smoke and drink, or people who believe differently. This may be fine for children, but teenagers shouldn't be overprotected from the real world. They need regular contact and interaction with people and cultures outside their comfort zones. While our three kids did attend Christian schools all the way through college, we tried to make sure they were not isolated from the outside world. We encouraged their exposure to environments that would challenge their thinking. Your kids need to learn how to be *in the world, but not of it* (see John 17:14–16)—just as Jesus was.

In light of this, why did we choose to send our children to Christian schools? We realized early that we had a choice. Did we want the *state* to educate our children or the *church*? It really came down to that. Who did we most trust to look out for the best interests of our kids? For us the decision was an easy one. We had an excellent Christian school system in our area, so we enrolled our kids there.

When our children were ready for junior high school, we allowed them to make their own choices. They could go on to the Christian junior high school or switch to the public junior high school. They chose the Christian junior high. I'm sure that their exposure to Christian school when they were young influenced their teenage decisions. Adolescents may be notorious risk-takers, but they generally don't like having their lives disrupted. I never recommend forcing teenagers to change schools unless they are having serious problems where they are.

What about Home-school?

The home-schooling movement continues to grow rapidly in North America, fueled largely by parental fears concerning the well-publicized

85

increase in school violence, the alleged acceptance of homosexuality as a lifestyle choice, the potential for negative peer influence, and other concerns.

Parents should choose to home-school their kids not based on fear but on what's best for their kids. If you have the time, training, and resources to provide your children with the best education possible, then home-school may be the best option. Parents who home-school teenagers also need to have a special relationship with their kids. It's not easy to be both a parent and teacher to a teenager.

I don't recommend home-schooling teenagers except for special situations with special-needs students. I believe most adolescents need the opportunity to learn from adults outside the home, particularly during adolescence when they are separating from their parents. Teens also need ample opportunities to develop their social and interpersonal skills and to test their new thinking and reasoning abilities on as many other people as possible.

But whether your kids attend a public school, a private school, a boarding school, or no school at all, make sure they learn all they can. School should not get in the way of their education.

Eliminate the
Homework Hassle

Go to your room, and don't you dare come out until your home-work is done! Don't you realize that your future is on the line? Or do you want to end up like your Uncle Fred? Do you?

Many parents today have somehow come to the conclusion that they, not their children, are the ones who are responsible for making sure they do well in school. They spend hours either nagging their kids about their homework or actually doing it for them. Most of these parents are pet-rified by the thought that their kids might fail or be held back in school. They fear what other people might think, or they fear that failure will cause their child to suffer from low self-esteem.

But low self-esteem doesn't come from failing or suffering the conse-quences of failing. On the contrary, failure has the potential to actually enhance a student's self-esteem if (1) they are given responsibility for over-coming that failure and (2) nobody else interferes in the process. We do kids no favors by rescuing them from their failures and mistakes. They learn best by trial and error, with the emphasis on the *error*. If you prevent the error, you prevent the learning. It's really that simple.

Stay Out of It

That's why I recommend that you resist getting involved in your kid's schoolwork. It's their responsibility, not yours. It's common these days for parents to work themselves into a "quality time" frenzy—supervising their kids' homework on a nightly basis, making sure that every assignment is done correctly and on time. Sometimes these parents actually go "back to school" themselves, heroically reading the textbooks and trying to learn the subject matter so that they can tutor their kids or, if all else fails, do their homework for them.

Don't do that! Don't try to be a hero. Your job is to monitor progress, to coach and encourage from the sidelines, and to hold your student accountable—but that's about it. Of course you care a great deal about how well your teen does in school, but you should also care enough to allow your teen to do it on his or her own. That's the only way they will truly benefit from their school experience.

While there are always exceptions, most teenagers—if they are left alone and not overly pushed by their parents—will do okay in school and require little supervision and extra motivation. Don't worry if your teenager isn't getting straight As or winning academic-achievement awards. It's not likely that you can turn your average student into an overachiever by nagging or pushing. In fact, the more you get involved, the greater the likelihood the student will do worse, not better. Remember, it's her job to get her education.

When Extra Motivation Is Needed

Most kids are motivated to do well in school by a combination of two things: *ambition* and *anxiety*.

Despite what some think about today's teenagers, most are pretty ambitious. They like challenges and enjoy the feeling of accomplishment that comes from getting good grades and pleasing their teachers and parents. Career ambitions or just a desire to excel at whatever they do may motivate others. Some kids are ambitious by nature, and others develop it gradually over time. It can be encouraged in teenagers by modeling it for them and by providing them with lots of affirmation rather than nagging. Your teenager probably is more ambitious than you realize, even if that ambition is not channeled directly into schoolwork.

Anxiety—or fear—is also a significant motivator. Most students fear what might happen if they don't do their schoolwork. They might be embarrassed in front of their classmates or put their future at risk or lose a scholarship or make their parents angry.

Ambition and anxiety work in tandem. One or the other usually provides the motivation necessary to make students out of most kids. But what if that doesn't happen? What if your teenager seems to lack both ambition *and* anxiety? What if he or she just doesn't care?

The answer is not to make their performance *your* problem, but *theirs*. Sometimes parents and teachers worry and fret about a student's poor grades while the student could care less. Unless your teenager cares as much (or more) than you do, he or she won't be motivated to change or to take responsibility for performing up to his or her capabilities.

The best solution is to make school performance something that your kids care about. You can't give them ambition they don't have, but you can increase their anxiety level by tying school performance to the privileges that they enjoy and/or expect. Most kids care a lot about having time with their friends, having money to spend, having a car to drive, participating in sports, or having additional freedom. If their bad grades translate into a loss of privileges, they'll start caring about their school performance. They'll start feeling some anxiety.

Most kids won't take kindly to this exercise of your authority. They will probably fight it tooth and nail at first. They'll act like they really don't care what you do to them and refuse to change just out of spite. They'll act like victims and try to blame you for ruining their lives. Don't fall for it. Just follow through and be patient. Eventually they will learn that you are serious and that if their situation is going to improve, they will be the ones who have to do the improving.

Of course, to make such a system work, you'll need some way of monitoring how your student is doing, preferably on a weekly basis. There is simply too much time between report cards. What you need to know is whether or not your son or daughter completed the work that was assigned to them for the week, whether or not they are getting an acceptable grade. Some parents make arrangements with teachers and administrators to use a simple form at the end each week (brought to school by the student on Friday), which asks teachers in each class to give a progress report, along with a signature to discourage student dishonesty.

Your objective is not to micromanage your teenager's life but to communicate clearly that they are in total control of their lives. They have responsibilities that they can choose to accept or ignore. The choices are theirs, just as the outcomes of their choices are also theirs. That's how real life works.

This may not be necessary for your kids. Keep in mind that some underachieving students may have significant learning disabilities that should be properly diagnosed and treated. But the best response for the vast majority of kids who lack the motivation to apply themselves at school is to simply back off and let them take responsibility for their own school performance. Make it matter to them. In most cases, they will turn things around on their own, and they will learn a valuable life lesson in the process.

Show Them What You Know

The more skills and responsibilities you can pass along to your kids, the better.

Daniels and Sons Jewelers
The Flying Wallendas
Brainerd, Brainerd, and Brainerd, Attorneys-at-Law
The Clark Family Experience
Ken Griffey Jr.
Levas and Son Furniture

In every walk of life, it's extremely common for children to take up the vocation of their parents. While you want to encourage your children to find their own niche, to be themselves, to not feel obligated to do what you do—there's a high probability that they will indeed walk in your footsteps.

Down through history, this was a very natural thing for young people to do. Children who grew up on farms became farmers themselves. The offspring of morticians became morticians. The children of circus performers became circus performers. There is a long tradition of passing skills and trades down from generation to generation. Parents of the past often raised children specifically to take over their family enterprise.

While it may not be as common today as it once was, we still see many young people who take up the vocations of their parents. We all know of politicians, actors, athletes, and musicians who literally inherited their life's work.

Two of my dad's three sons followed him in the business of being a building contractor. I probably would have gone into the building trades, but God had other ideas. I became a youth pastor, and my son is now also a youth pastor. Most kids look first to their parents for cues on what they want to become.

Even if you don't think your kids would want to do what you do as a career (or even if you don't want them to), they can still learn much from you that they can use later in life. If you're a plumber, then by all means teach your kids how to fix a leaky faucet. If you're a lawyer, teach them to write up a contract or file a lawsuit. If you're a car dealer, teach them how to get the best deal on a new car. If you're a golfer, teach them to play golf. If you're a stay-at-home mom, teach them to maintain a household. You have tons of experience that can at least be partially passed on to your kids. They'll not only be able to use the knowledge they get from you, but in the process they'll have some valuable time with you.

Although I didn't become a building contractor like my dad, I'll always be grateful to him for teaching me the basics of the building trades. That knowledge has saved me a good deal of money over the years doing jobs myself that most people have to hire someone else to do. Even today when I strap on my nail apron and tackle some little carpentry project around the house, I'm reminded of my dad and the times we spent building something together.

Parents As Mentors

When your kids become teenagers, you'll want to become less the parent and more the coach and consultant. Of course you'll always be Mom or Dad to your kids, but as they grow and mature, you can step out of that parenting role from time to time and assume the role of a mentor and teacher.

A great way to start making that transition is to identify a few skills or abilities of yours that you can pass along to your kids, some knowledge that would be of value to them. Teach your son or daughter how to fly-fish, silkscreen a poster, back a trailer, lubricate a car, cook a turkey, or operate a chain saw. These experiences put you in a much better position to coach and counsel your kids on important matters concerning values, personal conduct, faith, and decision making. Kids who come to appreciate their parents' guidance and direction in the little things are more likely to appreciate their parents' guidance and direction in the big things.

Passing the Baton

Some time ago I learned a simple four-step process for transferring skills or responsibilities to others called the "Four Phases of Ease." By using this process, or one like it, you can teach anyone (including your kids) how to do what you do. It is based on the idea that you don't want to discourage students by dumping too much responsibility on them too soon, nor do you want to discourage them by not giving them enough responsibility when they are ready for it. Used properly, the Four Phases of Ease can help you pass the baton to your son or daughter. Here's how it works:

• Phase One: I do it; you watch.

Let's say you want to teach your son or daughter to trim the rosebushes. "Hey, Michael, would you mind keeping me company for a few minutes while I trim the roses out front? I could really use somebody to talk to." Chances are Michael will watch, ask questions, and perhaps show some interest in what you're doing.

• Phase Two: We do it together.

"Michael, I could really use your help trimming the rosebushes this afternoon. I picked up an extra pair of clippers and gloves you can use. Afterward, we'll go get some frozen yogurt." Okay, you may need to bribe him a little bit. Since he has watched you do it, he's probably willing to give it a try.

• Phase Three: You do it; I watch.

"Michael, thanks so much for helping me trim the rosebushes today. You did a great job. I noticed that you cut them back a little more than we did last time, but I'm sure they'll survive and grow back. Let's watch the next few weeks and see how they do." This phase allows him to do more on his own while you offer feedback and coaching.

• Phase Four. You do it; I go do something else.

"Michael, I'd really appreciate it if you would take responsibility for keeping the rosebushes trimmed. That would be a huge contribution to our family. If you'll agree to do that, it will help out a lot. Thanks."

It's a simple process, but it works. Michael may not trim the rosebushes on schedule, and he may grumble about it when he does, but at least he won't blame it on his lack of ability. And someday, he'll be glad he knows how to trim roses. One of these days, when he has a home of his own, he'll probably have the loveliest front yard on his street.

The more skills and responsibilities you can pass along to your kids, the better. Kids who are considered most at-risk are those kids who suffer from low self-esteem—they don't believe they are capable of doing anything very well. You can increase your son's or daughter's feelings of self-confidence and self-worth by passing along to them some of the skills that you have developed.

Give Their Dreams
Some Direction

Whatever you do, work at it with all your heart, as working for the Lord, not for men . . . It is the Lord Christ you are serving.
—Colossians 3:23–24

When Aaron was a sophomore in high school, he won first prize in an essay contest for high-school students sponsored by the local newspaper. His essay was titled "All God's Children" and dealt with the topic of race relations from a Christian perspective. After it was published in the paper, he received dozens of congratulatory phone calls and letters from people all over the country who had read his essay and encouraged him to keep writing.

Aaron began to dream about someday becoming a successful Christian author or perhaps the editor of a major Christian magazine like *Christianity Today* or maybe a columnist or religion editor for a major daily newspaper.

But Aaron had few outlets for developing his writing talent. There were no more essay contests to enter. He didn't take steps on his own to learn more about the publishing business, pursue an internship at the paper, or join the staff of the school newspaper. He didn't enroll in a writing or religion course outside of school; he just concentrated on getting good grades in preparation for college.

Aaron's parents spent little time talking with him about how he might pursue his dream of becoming a Christian journalist, but they did spend a lot of time making sure he got into the "right" college. They narrowed their choices based on the reputation of the school, location, tuition costs, Aaron's SAT and ACT scores, his junior-class ranking and GPA, and his interest in writing. They visited most of the colleges on their list and began submitting applications. Several very good schools accepted him, but since he was offered a partial scholarship to his father's alma mater, a small college in the Midwest, he decided to enroll there.

Aaron soon discovered that this college offered few courses in journalism. He majored in English at first, but finding the classes to be difficult, he switched to communications. That didn't suit him either, so he changed his major to business, at the urging of his father. Now, in his junior year, he feels that he has made some bad choices. He's not sure he went to the right college after all, and he's uncertain about what he wants to do. He's worried that when he graduates he won't be able to get the job he wants—or any job at all.

Aaron's situation is typical of many young people today. They have big dreams but little direction. They know where they want to go, but they don't know how to get there. With a diploma in hand, Aaron will undoubtedly find a job that will provide him with a decent income, but it's unlikely that he will ever become the Christian journalist he wanted to become.

Where Do They Want to Go?

Despite what you hear to the contrary, today's teenagers have big dreams. Some say they are the most ambitious generation in history. They have grown up in a world that has exploded with possibilities. They are better informed and more aware of what's going on in the world than any preceding generation. Advertisers appeal to their ambitious spirit with slogans like "Where do you want to go today?" and "Just do it!"

The vast majority of kids today have their sights set on becoming physicians, lawyers, artists, entertainers, high-tech entrepreneurs, and business managers. Very few want to work as machinists, construction workers, secretaries, or soldiers. According to recent studies, more than 90 percent of all kids—rich, poor, Asian, black, Hispanic, and white—plan to attend college and work in professional, high-paying jobs.

But while they are ambitious, they often have no direction. Their dreams are rarely connected to specific educational and career goals. Because today's kids spend so much time in school, and because there's so much pressure on them to get good grades, they are mistakenly led to believe that school is all that's required. Just get your education. That college diploma is your ticket to success. Going to school becomes the primary objective rather than the pursuit of a specific vocation or calling in life.

No wonder so many young people are graduating from college with degrees that are basically useless to them. Their time and their parents' money probably would have been better spent elsewhere. A college diploma is no longer the Holy Grail it used to be. Unless students know where they are going and how they will get there, it's unlikely they will arrive at the right destination. Ask any of the college graduates who are working behind the cosmetic counters of department stores or driving furniture delivery trucks.

Helping Them Get There

What is your teenager's dream? Would you like to help him or her pursue it? Here are some things you can do:

1. *Start talking.* While little children like to play "when I grow up," teenagers sometimes have to be coaxed into sharing their ambitions, hopes, and dreams with anyone else. You don't want to push your kids prematurely or to put additional pressure on them, but you can give them a hopeful vision of the future that will inspire and motivate them.
2. *Be supportive.* Even if your son's or daughter's dreams seem unrealistic or are not what you had in mind for them, try to be as positive and supportive as possible. If they have chosen the wrong course, they'll find that out soon enough. When kids have their dreams crushed, they are less likely to dream again.
3. *Offer ideas.* Many kids have no idea what they want to do as a career. They may only know what they enjoy doing now, what subjects in school they like, or in what they excel. You can offer ideas and suggestions and point them toward careers that match up well with their ambitions and abilities.
4. *Develop a life plan.* Think through some of the steps that might be

required to achieve your teenager's goals, and come up with a rough timetable and process for accomplishing them. "What can I do? How can I get more experience? Who can I talk to? What classes should I take? What schools specialize in this area? Are there internships available?" Contrary to what some kids think, things don't just happen. If they have a life plan, they are more apt to "get a life."

5. *Monitor progress.* Don't develop a life plan and then forget about it. Continue to explore ways for your kids to pursue their ambitions. Keep talking; keep encouraging. Don't worry if they get discouraged, have doubts, or change direction a few times. Given the rapidly changing nature of the world, new careers seem to spring up every day. But it's best to be moving toward something.

Vocational Training

When I talk to teenagers about the future, I like to help them understand the difference between their *vocation* and their *occupation.*

Their vocation is their *calling*, what God has called them to do. All of us have been called to serve God, to glorify Him, to honor Him (see Isaiah 43:7). Or as the Westminster Catechism puts it, "The chief end of man is to glorify God and to enjoy him forever." That's why we were created.

Their occupation, on the other hand, is how they fulfill their vocation. God has given all of us gifts and talents and abilities that we can use to serve Him in whatever occupation we choose. You don't have to go into the ministry to serve God. As Paul wrote, "Whatever you do, work at it with all your heart, as working for the Lord, not for men . . . It is the Lord Christ you are serving" (Colossians 3:23–24). We can serve God anywhere.

Christian youth often worry about God's will for their lives. But we already know what God's will is. It is to serve Him in whatever we do. Teens should feel free to pursue their dreams and ambitions knowing that they will always be in God's will if they are willing to serve Him. There are no unemployment lines in the Kingdom of God.

Make Chores
Mandatory

So the LORD God banished him from the Garden of Eden to work the
ground from which he had been taken.

—Genesis 3:23

B ut you don't understand. I have my life to live, and there are things that
are important to me. Mowing the lawn is not one of them. If it's so
important to my dad, why can't he just do it himself? He knows how much
I hate it. Besides, he always wants me to do it when I want to do something
else. Being with my friends may not seem very important to him, but it is to
me. The grass isn't going to die if I don't mow it right now. Doesn't he
remember what it was like to be my age? I'll bet he wanted to be with his
friends instead of having to milk the cows or whatever it was his old man
bugged him about all the time."

◆ ◆ ◆

There may be a few kids who do chores regularly without griping—but
not many. As long as there have been parents and children, there have been
hassles over chores. When God banished Adam and Eve from paradise and
made them start working for a living (Genesis 3:23), that's surely when the
grumbling started.

In the past, children probably grumbled less and contributed more mainly
because there was a greater need for their help. But with the increase in labor-
saving devices today and the shift from living on farms to living in cities and
suburbs, the need for raising children as workers has significantly decreased.

Children aren't expected to do much around the house anymore. In many families, chores have become all but obsolete—a trend that has unfortunately contributed to the inability of many kids to assume the responsibilities of adulthood. Ever wonder why kids from rural America seem more mature and self-reliant than kids from the cities and suburbs? In most cases, it's because they have had chores to do.

Three Cheers for Chores

You owe it to your kids to make chores mandatory. Here are a few reasons why:

Chores endow kids with skills they'll need to lead successful adult lives. Domestic skills are no less important than any others. Everybody needs to learn how to wash, iron, and fold their own clothes, prepare meals, run a vacuum cleaner, take care of pets, scrub floors, mow grass, weed a garden, polish brass, wash a car, rake leaves, clean toilets, shovel snow, and remove dust from furniture. If kids are doing such things regularly at home, they will not only learn these skills, but they'll learn to appreciate the effort that their parents put forth to provide and maintain a home for them. This is something they might otherwise take for granted.

Chores increase a young person's sense of significance. Everyone needs to feel needed, and kids are no exception. In the past, kids knew they were an important part of the family because they were contributors to it. They were considered assets instead of liabilities. Your kids may not have cows to milk, but they can be given age-appropriate responsibilities around the house to make them feel more connected to the family as a participant. Doing so will build on their feelings of worth and self-esteem. If their chores are legitimate, necessary, and appreciated by the rest of the family, they will probably do them without objection. After all, it feels good to know that you are needed.

Chores build character. Kids who grow up without having to do any of the dirty work around the house are more likely to look down upon those who do. They may develop an attitude of superiority, believing that mundane tasks or work without pay is below them and only for those who aren't smart enough to avoid it. Kids who do chores, however, are likely to be less selfish and more apt to develop a servant's heart. Good citizenship begins at home, and when kids learn to give back to their families, they will be more likely to give back to their community, their country, and their God.

Chores provide opportunities for kids to learn responsibility. They learn to fulfill obligations, honor commitments, and meet deadlines. They learn to arrange their lives in such a way that they will be able to do both what they want to do *and* what they have to do. They learn that work has worthwhile benefits. Kids who never have to lift a finger to receive all the amenities of life learn soon enough that anything can be had for nothing. That's a powerful message sent to children by parents who make no demands on them whatsoever.

Making Chores Work

It's never easy to get kids to do chores or to eliminate all the hassles associated with them, but there are a few things you can do to make them work better in your family.

1. Start giving your kids chores when they are young. Even a three-year-old is capable of picking clothes up off the floor or putting away toys. Kids who had chores as children are more likely to do them as teenagers without complaining.

2. If you or your kids don't like the sound of the word *chores,* call them something else, like *contributions* or *family service.* At our house, we just called them *responsibilities.*

3. Assign chores to everyone in the family, including parents. Teenagers aren't servants, so don't make them do all the things you don't want to do.

4. Make sure everyone knows exactly what his or her chore is, how it is to be done, and when it should be completed. Be specific and reasonable.

5. Don't punish kids by assigning them chores.

6. Make sure your teen has (or knows how to get) all they need to complete the job successfully. For example, if his job is to mow the lawn, make sure he has a lawn mower that works properly and that he has been instructed on how to use and maintain it. Try to help your teen be as self-sufficient as possible in his or her chores.

7. Don't do your teen's chores for him or her, even though it may be convenient to do so. That will only encourage your teen to wait and see if

you'll do it again next time. Avoid doing someone else's job unless you are asked to do so or a special situation requires it.

8. Make chores age-appropriate. Teenagers can and should do something more meaningful than take out the trash. They can help with laundry, meal preparation, taking care of pets, automobiles, lawns, gardens, and family finances.

9. Let kids have some choice or flexibility in the chores they do and in how they do them. Example: "The family room, hall, and bedrooms need vacuuming once a week. You can do it on Monday, Tuesday, or Wednesday. Your choice."

10. Give each person in the family his or her own chores rather than assigning shared chores. This will reduce arguing, finger pointing and blaming when the chore isn't done.

11. Create a family chore chart if that helps. All chores are listed with the names of those responsible and can be checked off when done. This monitors progress and completion.

12. Don't pay kids to do chores. It's better to give them a set allowance (a portion of the family income), separate from chores. If you pay kids to do chores, then they won't do the chore unless they need money.

13. Connect chores with privileges and consequences. Kids need to learn that privileges come with responsibilities. If your teenager doesn't want the responsibility, then he or she will be faced with giving up a corresponding privilege.

14. Don't expect perfection. Resist the temptation to "fix" a finished chore even though you know you could do a better job.

15. Learn to *delegate and distance yourself*. Don't hover over your kids or pester them about when they are going to get the chore done. Just be clear about what, how, and when, then leave them alone. If they fail to complete the job by the agreed-upon time, they simply lose a privilege or suffer a consequence.

16. Always show appreciation when a chore has been completed. Everyone likes to know that his or her efforts have not gone unnoticed.

17. Give your kids some constructive feedback they can use next time. Coach rather than criticize the work they do, offering suggestions and ideas for improving their work.

Hang in There

Accept the fact that chores may not get done, may get done poorly, or may become a constant source of hassling. You may have to continually nag your kids to get them done—but don't quit trying.

One of our son Corey's chores was to put our trash barrels at the end of our long driveway every week so that they would get picked up by the trash collectors. I always had to ride him about doing that; it seemed like a constant battle of two wills, his against mine. It got so bad that I was tempted to take those garbage cans and dump the contents on his bed just to make my point. This went on for months, maybe years.

But one day I suddenly realized that several weeks had gone by without my having to remind him or scold him for not getting those trash cans out there. Had all the nagging finally paid off? Did I finally win? Actually, I think it had more to do with Corey's growing up than anything else. As he got older, he simply matured and got to the point where his own sense of responsibility prevailed over his childish need to avoid work at all costs. He just made a decision to go ahead and take care of those trash cans for us, and it became a habit.

Build Their Tolerance for Frustration

Frustration is essential for healthy character formation and emotional strength.

I know I spend too much money on my kids, but I don't apologize for that. I may not be able to give them what they need, but I can give them what they want. Besides, it makes me feel good to see them happy."

◆ ◆ ◆

The busy dad who made that comment is not alone in his thinking. There are many frustrated parents today who resort to giving their kids everything they want because they don't have the time or strength of will to give them what they really need. They lavishly indulge their kids in an attempt to make their lives as comfortable and painless and stress-free as possible.

Sounds like what you would do for a person on his or her deathbed, not someone who still has an entire life to live.

The Dreaded F Word

"Don't frustrate your children," taught the first wave of child-rearing psychologists. They taught that frustration is bad for children, that it causes insecurity, unhappiness, and low self-esteem in children—not to mention extensive damage to the vocal cords from inordinate amounts of screaming.

So parents did everything they could to spare their children frustration.

They gave them everything they wanted, when they wanted it, requiring little or nothing from them in return. In the process, they managed to raise an entire generation of selfish, spoiled, demanding, and ungrateful kids.

Truth is, frustration isn't bad for children at all. It's essential for healthy character formation and emotional strength. Through experience with frustration, children eventually develop a tolerance for it, accept its inevitability, and learn to cope with it. Those who develop a tolerance for frustration have the ability to turn adversity into challenge and persevere in the face of it.

All of us are familiar with the success stories of great men and women in history who overcame great obstacles in life in order to achieve seemingly impossible goals. While we are inspired by the perseverance and courage demonstrated by these heroic people, we sometimes don't realize that these qualities weren't handed to them on a silver platter. In most cases, they acquired them by being seriously deprived of most of the amenities of life that today's kids routinely receive as a matter of course.

Point-and-Click Kids

It's no wonder so many young people today have a hard time accepting adult responsibility. Kids who grow up in a blissful state of premature affluence find it hard to accept that they may no longer be entitled to the same comforts they enjoyed as children. No wonder so many young adults choose to live with their parents even after they have found jobs. Why spend your own money on food and housing when you can spend it on cool stuff like new cars, nice clothes, expensive stereo equipment, ski trips, and fast computers. They don't want to have to start at the bottom and work their way up.

Marketers sometimes call today's youth the point-and-click generation, a reference to their having grown up believing that anything they want is available with a click of the mouse. Point-and-click kids believe that nothing is off-limits to them; they believe they are entitled to everything they want whenever they want it. This is not a completely new phenomenon, of course, but in the past it was limited to children of the superrich. Today it has trickled down to the lower middle class. Parents don't have to be rich to overindulge their kids today.

Why We Do It

No one intentionally handicaps their children by giving them too much. Overindulged kids are usually raised by good, well-meaning parents who have worked hard for what they have. They love their kids and just want to share with them the hard-won fruits of their labor. Good reasons abound for overindulgence.

Some parents fear confrontation or conflict with their kids. Of course, kids sense this vulnerability and seize it as a way to apply pressure and demand more and more. If they don't get what they want, they punish parents with additional anger, pouting, or withdrawal, shifting all the power in the family to the child.

Emotionally needy parents may fear rejection. They believe their kids will like them more if they shower them with things and grant their every wish. In reality, kids are more likely to learn that their parents are weak and easily manipulated. They may use overindulgence as a way to bribe their kids or win them over. This happens frequently when there are marital conflicts, differences in parenting styles, or divorced parents attempting to buy their children's loyalty.

Harried and overworked parents often don't have the emotional energy to deal with kids who whine, nag, and pester them for the things they want. They give in rather than stand up for what they know is the right thing to do. Other busy parents feel guilty for not giving their kids enough time or attention, so they attempt to reduce their guilt by giving material things.

Some parents can't resist "keeping up with the Joneses." If the neighbor's kid gets a new bike or a new computer or a new Mercedes-Benz, the pressure is on. It's not easy to teach kids to resist peer pressure when parents can't handle it.

Just Say No

Maybe if parents learned to say no more often, kids would too.

"But my kids won't take no for an answer." Maybe that's because they don't hear it enough to understand what it means.

Kids with a healthy tolerance for frustration understand that no is neither an unreasonable nor unexpected response to many of the demands they make on others. Sometimes they will get a yes (for which they can be grateful), but they don't require it nor feel overly distraught when they don't get it.

No is actually one of the most character-building words in the English language. It provides young people with an opportunity to either overcome adversity or learn to live with it. Children whose parents aren't afraid to say no eventually discover that things don't always go their way. Sometimes they have to adapt and adjust to setbacks without taking everything personally or attacking those who are responsible for those setbacks. They learn both perseverance and resourcefulness, two very important qualities of character.

Parents shouldn't say no to their kids all the time, in every situation, nor should they fight needless battles over unimportant issues. Teenagers can become resentful and rebellious when their parents aren't willing to listen and grant reasonable requests.

But if your kids start expecting you to provide them with whatever they want, whenever and however they want it, you need to say no with conviction and strength. If you constantly cave in to the demands of your kids, even when they are cloaked in syrupy hugs, kisses, and tears, you will absolutely guarantee manipulative, self-centered kids. Learn to say no and help your young adult develop a healthy tolerance for frustration and the confidence to overcome the challenges of life.

Less Is More

When my kids were little, I got into the habit of bringing home a gift or two for them when I was traveling. Quite by accident I stumbled upon a principle that I now recommend to others. *Never give your kids more than one gift at a time.* If you give them one, they will usually treasure it. If you give them *two,* they will only look for a third.

Don't get me wrong. I'm not against giving gifts to children. Our heavenly Father is a generous giver of gifts (James 1:17), but rarely does He give us more than we need. I love to give my children gifts, but I have learned to be careful in doing so. Giving them too much may actually be giving them too little of what they really need to become successful in life.

Resist the Urge
to Rescue

Allow for mistakes. That's the only way learning can take place.

A young man was appointed president of a bank. Seeking some counsel, he approached the venerable old chairman of the board, "Sir, I respect your wisdom. Can you give me some advice on how to be a successful bank president?"

The old man thought about it for a moment and replied, "Make wise decisions."

The young man said, "How do I learn how to make wise decisions?"

"Get some experience," said the old man.

The young man said, "Thank you, sir, that's very helpful. But I don't have much experience right now. When will I have enough experience to make wise decisions?"

The old man said, "When you have made enough foolish ones."

Wouldn't it be nice if you could learn without making mistakes? Like it or not, there's no other way. That's why somebody invented the flight simulator. For those rare endeavors (like flying airplanes) where even one mistake can be fatal, there still has to be a way to allow for mistakes. That's the only way learning can take place.

Thomas Edison, the inventor of the light bulb, reportedly made an astonishing nine hundred light bulbs that didn't work before he finally made one that did. With each failure, he learned one more way not to make a light bulb.

Nobody's Perfect

Failures often point to success. Some of the most valuable lessons in life can only be learned through the process of trial and error. That is especially true for teenagers. It's better for kids to make mistakes under the supervision and mentoring of parents than to make them later in life when no one will care whether they learn from them or not.

You can count on teenagers making lots of mistakes. Unless you have an approval junkie, a zombie, or a robot, teens will mess up frequently. They will test the limits, act without thinking, do or say stupid things, and get into plenty of trouble.

Which is the key to effective learning—getting into trouble. Mistakes alone don't always teach, but consequences do. Unless a mistake has a consequence—a bit of trouble—there's no logical reason to avoid the mistake.

It's natural for us to want to protect our kids from consequences, to save them (and us) a lot of trouble, but it's important to remember that consequences are in most cases good for them. They not only teach specific lessons concerning the behavior in question, but they build self-esteem. They teach kids that what they do matters, that they have power over their environment, that they can control their destinies. It's up to them. They have the power to make good or bad things happen. They are not victims of circumstances but agents of change.

Kids who never learn about natural consequences will have a great deal of difficulty later in life. They tend to believe that everything is out of their control, that nothing is ever their fault. They feel like victims, that "stuff happens," and there is nothing they can do to improve or change a situation. These are the kids who are most vulnerable to negative peer pressure and irresponsible behaviors.

Parents As Lifeguards

Most behaviors have natural consequences. They happen naturally unless someone interferes. If you eat spoiled food, you are likely to get sick. If you go out in the rain without a raincoat or umbrella, you will get wet. If you lose your jacket, you will be cold.

With so many potential consequences out there, our tendency as parents is to play lifeguard. Either we don't allow our kids near the deep end (we overprotect), or we jump in the water and pull them out as soon as they start to sink (we rescue). We do this not because we are bad parents, but because we are good parents. We love our kids and don't want them to be sick, wet, or cold.

Sometimes we rescue simply because old habits are hard to break. We've been rescuing our kids since the day they were born. But while it's necessary to change a baby's messy diaper, it is not always necessary to clean up the mess of a teenager.

Remember when your little boy or girl went off to school without his or her lunch? Like most good parents, you probably jumped in the car and delivered the lunch.

It took a few years, but my wife and I finally decided to stop delivering our children's forgotten lunches. These incidents had increased in frequency despite our constant reminders and warnings. We realized that the problem was no longer theirs, but ours. Every time we delivered a lunch, we were probably also sending the message, "See how your parents love you? Whenever you mess up, we'll clean it up. If you are irresponsible, no problem. We will always come to your rescue." This was not a message that we wanted to continue sending.

Besides, we read somewhere that it takes an average of sixty-five days for people to starve to death. None of our kids did.

It was hard to resist rescuing—not only because we didn't want our kids to suffer, but also because we didn't want people to think badly about us. But by transferring the responsibility for remembering lunch to our kids, they learned to take full responsibility for getting all their stuff to school—books, backpacks, jackets, and anything else they needed. If they did forget something, it was their responsibility to deal with it. If they really needed something badly, they could call us and ask us to deliver the forgotten item (which we were usually willing to do), but they had to make the call. It was their responsibility.

Of course, there are times when parents *should* rescue their kids from experiencing natural consequences, such as when a child runs out into the street. No one would advise letting an oncoming car hit the child so that he or she could learn from the experience. Sometimes natural consequences are too severe and intervention is required. These are generally exceptions, however, and not the rule.

Big-Time Crime

When I was in the ninth grade, I was caught shoplifting. I hate to admit it, but at the time, I was something of a kleptomaniac. Several of my friends and I would go into stores and steal things just for the thrill of it. One day we were caught in the act, and police were called to the scene. We were actually handcuffed and rode in the backseat of a patrol car to the police station, where our parents were summoned to come and pick us up. Charges were filed, and we eventually had to go to juvenile court.

To my parents' credit, they didn't yell and scream at me or tell me how terrible I was. I knew that already. It was obvious from the hurt on their faces and the tears in their eyes that I had let them down big-time. This made a big impression on me.

Actually, I don't remember ever being punished by my parents for what I did. They didn't confine me to my room or take away all my privileges. Instead, they simply resisted the urge to interfere when the judge put us on a year's probation and sentenced us to pay back all of the merchants from whom we had stolen merchandise. The amount of money was considerable, and it took me a long time to earn it, not to mention the humiliation of walking into every single one of those stores, apologizing to the store manager, and personally handing over the money. This was a condition of my sentence.

I haven't shoplifted since. I was no Einstein, but I learned my lesson well. My parents could have paid off every one of those stores in a flash and probably could have saved me a lot of embarrassment and disgrace, but they didn't. They didn't rescue. They let me clean up my own mess.

The great thing about natural consequences is that you don't have to think them up or do anything to make them work. In fact, if you do anything at all, you ruin their effectiveness. Natural consequences just *are*. If your teenager blows all his allowance on some impulsive purchase and then comes to you begging for more money so he can go to a concert with his friends, the best thing to do is nothing at all. Sure, you can empathize with his situation and help him learn from it, but you must resist the urge to rescue. If he doesn't go to the concert and is upset . . . he has no reason to be upset at you. He's learning something very important about himself. His feeling upset for one night is small potatoes compared to someday not being able to pay his income taxes or house payment.

Remember to give your kids full responsibility for their own problems. Parents should never agonize over teenage behavior when teenagers are perfectly capable of agonizing over it themselves.

Teach Them the Truth about Consequences

Kids need to learn that the real world operates by laws of cause and effect that can't be suspended just because they are inconvenient.

Hardly any task of parenthood is more challenging than discipline. Most people equate it with punishment. But the goal of discipline is not punishment. Its primary purpose is to build character—to help kids become more mature and independent. Punishment is something that someone in power does to someone else, usually to condemn or seek retribution. But discipline is not like that. We don't do it *to* teenagers but *with* them to insure that they learn to become responsible, self-disciplined adults. While discipline is positive, punishment rarely is.

So how do you discipline teenagers? They're too big to spank. Screaming, yelling, and threatening don't work.

The best way to discipline teenagers is by consistently and rationally connecting behavior with consequences.

Logical Consequences

Natural consequences were discussed in the previous chapter. With natural consequences, the parent's role is minimal. All you have to do is allow the situation to happen without intervention.

But *logical* consequences require you to get involved, to exercise some authority. They don't happen naturally. They are created by parents, or when possible by parents and teens together, and are generally applied when the following conditions exist:

- *Unavailable natural consequences.* For example, there are no natural consequences for violating curfew. The car won't stop running, nobody turns into a pumpkin, nothing bad happens (hopefully). This, therefore, calls for another (logical) consequence that you'll have to decide with your teenager ahead of time.
- *Unacceptable natural consequences.* If your teenager takes the family car to a party and gets drunk, the natural consequence (driving home and getting into a fatal accident) is unacceptable. You must intervene if you can and impose logical consequences.
- *Ineffective natural consequences.* For example, if a teenager goofs off and doesn't study for his history final, the natural consequence (flunking the test) may not be effective enough to influence his or her future behavior.

Making the Connection

Here's how logical consequences work:

Whenever you set limits or make agreements with your teenager regarding behavior or expectations, you also need to discuss with him what happens in the event there is a failure to comply. If this is done before the fact, rather than after, it can be done without emotion, without struggle, without disagreement. If the consequence is reasonable, your teenager will likely understand the need for it and agree to it without argument. If he or she can't agree to a logical consequence, then you have reason to believe that your teenager has no intention of compliance anyway.

Logical consequences are best understood as a way of balancing privileges with responsibility. For the privilege of using the family car, there are consequences for not coming home at the agreed-upon time. For the privilege of having a wardrobe of clothes, there are consequences for not picking them up and putting them away.

Once logical consequences are in place, as with natural consequences, they should be allowed to take effect without parental intervention. Once they are established, there is no need for further disciplinary action. The consequence should itself provide the discipline.

Three Rs of Logical Consequences

The object of logical consequences is to teach responsibility. Once logical consequences become punishment, retribution, or vengeance, they lose their effectiveness. To prevent their misuse, authors H. Stephen Glenn and Jane Nelson suggest remembering the three Rs of logical consequences:

1. *They should be RELATED to the behavior in question.* In other words, the first place to look for a suitable consequence for a behavior is the behavior itself. Rather than grounding kids for every bad thing they do or using some other one-size-fits-all consequence, try connecting the behavior with the consequence in some logical way. If your teenager can't return the car with a full tank of gas, he loses driving privileges or has to wash the car the next day or get up early the next morning and get the gas tank filled at his expense. If she can't turn the volume down on her stereo after a certain hour, she loses her stereo or has her CD collection confiscated. It's impossible to make *every* logical consequence logical, but that's usually the best way to make them effective.

2. *They should be REASONABLE.* If a consequence is too severe or too harsh, teenagers are likely to become angry and resentful and rebel against it. While no consequence ever seems *fair* to a teenager, they will be more likely to accept them and learn from them if they make sense. Sometimes parents make the mistake of imposing consequences that are not only unreasonable but also unenforceable. "Either change your behavior or find another place to live!" They know you aren't serious when you say something like that. On the other hand, consequences shouldn't be so *inconsequential* that they don't act as a motivator or deterrent at all. If a teen's consequence for coming home from a party with alcohol on his breath is a $20 fine, the teenager is likely to think that's not a bad deal. Minor behaviors should result in minor consequences, serious behaviors in serious consequences. This will help teenagers understand values and choices in their proper perspective.

115

3. *They should be RESPECTFUL.* What this means is that we implement and enforce consequences out of a desire to help our kids become capable and responsible, not out of a desire to see our kids suffer, to get revenge, or to *win*. Again, our objective is not to punish, but to provide adequate and effective discipline.

Teenagers care deeply about fairness and respect. Even though they cry "unfair" at every opportunity, they do have the ability to understand why you must set limits and enforce consequences. Most kids will reluctantly admit that they respect and admire teachers at school who are clear and consistent with their requirements and rules, even though they have a hard time living up to them.

Making Them Work

One way to implement consequences respectfully is to present them as choices. Choices offer teenagers the opportunity to learn to make good decisions. "Either drive the speed limit, or we will drive you where you need to go." "Either feed your dog, or we will give the dog away." Obviously, logical consequences presented as choices have to be implemented ahead of time.

Let's say your teenager wants to go out with friends this weekend. That's fine, but when will he be home? You don't want to worry (which is your parental right), so you agree on when he should come home and a corresponding logical consequence. "Be home by midnight or stay home for the next three weeks. Your choice."

With such an arrangement, you don't need to worry, and your teenager can go out and have a good time. It's a win-win.

But what happens if your teenager doesn't come home on time? Do you get mad? Do you punish? Do you nag and lecture?

All you have to do is greet the teenager at the door and say, "I'm so glad you made it home safely. I was worried since you agreed to be home by midnight."

But you might add, "However, I'm surprised that you chose to stay home for the next three weeks. I want you to know that I respect your decision, and I'll make sure your wishes are granted."

Will your teenager then get angry or upset? You bet—but not at you. After all, you had nothing to do with this unfortunate outcome. Your teenager was completely in control and was the only one responsible. Will he learn? Again, you bet—but only if you treat your teenager with respect rather than with hostility and revenge. There's really no need to add insult to injury.

I admit that this example is an oversimplification. There are always extenuating circumstances, complications, and emotions are likely to run high. But if you can stay calm, remain objective, and use logical consequences as reasonably and rationally as you can, you can rest assured that your kids will be disciplined properly and learn from their mistakes. Remember that Rome wasn't built in a day. It often takes quite a few mistakes before the understanding dawns.

It will probably take some time for you to learn to use logical consequences effectively. It's much more an art than a science. You'll probably make some mistakes and have to feel your way along as you decide when to use consequences, how often you will use them, and what exactly they will be. Some kids will require that you use them a lot; others won't. Some require very severe consequences; others don't. You'll have to be creative and use your best judgment.

But remember, kids can get pretty creative too. They will resist and test your resolve. They'll come up with all kinds of excuses and reasons why they should be let off the hook. That's why it's important to be consistent, avoid manipulation, stay focused, and not let emotions take over. Your kids need to learn that the real world operates by laws of cause and effect that can't be suspended just because they are inconvenient. The consistent application of logical consequences will help teens learn this principle.

Limit Actions,
Not Attitudes

Young people have always been driven to challenge authority and assert themselves by being argumentative and unreasonable.

"Kristin, it's time to set the table for supper."

"I can't. I'm talking to Leanne on the phone. Get Jeffrey to do it."

"Jeffrey is doing his homework. It's your turn to set the table tonight."

"No! I'm on the phone!"

"Kristin, get in here right now and set the table, or you won't be talking to anyone on the phone for the next month!"

"MOM! The stupid table can wait. I have a life, you know! Maybe you should get one too, and you would understand!"

"Kristin, that was uncalled for."

"I hate living in this house! I hate you!"

❖ ❖ ❖

With that, Kristin abruptly hung up the phone, ran to her room in tears, and slammed the door. Kristin's mom was shaken, but she decided not to follow her daughter or to try to get in a last word. She wasn't sure what to do.

About twenty minutes later, Kristin emerged from her room and found her mother in the family room, still upset.

"Mom, I'll set the table now. Oh, after supper, could you take Tiffany and me to the mall? Her mom said she would bring us home."

"What?"

"I said I'll set the table, and can you give me and Tiffany a ride to the mall?"

"I can't believe you! How dare you come in here and ask me to take you to the mall after what you said to me?"

"Well, I didn't mean it."

Believe it or not, she's probably telling the truth. Teenagers—especially teenage girls—can get very upset, be very unkind, and then get over it very quickly. What teenagers say when they are mad often means nothing more than "I'm mad." The reason Kristin can ask her mother to take her to the mall twenty minutes after a major blowup is because in Kristin's mind, the exchange of words she had with her mom is over. It's ancient history. She's not mad anymore and is actually surprised that her mom still is.

Dealing with the volatile emotions and verbal tirades of teenagers can be a constant challenge for parents. We sometimes wonder why kids today aren't more like the Beaver and Wally Cleavers of a generation or two ago—when young people were pleasant, respectful, and polite. But that image of teenagers is just as much a myth as the one that stereotypes all of today's teenagers as criminally insane.

Young people have always been driven to challenge authority and assert themselves by being argumentative and unreasonable. The difference between now and then is that today's kids are encouraged and emboldened by popular culture and changing standards to be more abrasive and defiant of authority.

If Beaver or Wally had used the kind of coarse language that some kids use today in front of their parents, each would have had a bar of Ivory soap firmly inserted into their oral cavities. But punishment of that sort today is considered barbaric and abusive—and kids know it.

Roller-Coaster Emotions

Teenagers can get pretty worked up emotionally. There's a world of difference between the emotions of a child and the emotions of an adolescent. As a teen's mind and body develops, so does the intensity and immediacy of their emotions. Anger, embarrassment, anxiety, fear, elation, and infatuation

119

are rarely experienced or managed in moderation. When teenagers get mad or upset, they are likely to just let their feelings fly.

Adults are more apt to control their emotions, to differentiate between what they are feeling and the reality that may have generated those feelings. But teenagers aren't always able to make that distinction. The only reality they know is what they are feeling.

Teenagers are also well-known for their moodiness—the unpredictability and instability of their emotions. If you don't like your teenager's demeanor right now, just wait a little while; it will probably change. They may be feeling terrible one minute and wonderful the next. It's difficult to predict how they will feel from one moment to another. Of course, every teenager is different.

So it's best not to overreact or to take things too personally when your teenager is upset or angry. Don't let their bad day ruin yours. Try to empathize and remember that you probably drove your own parents nuts with the same kind of behavior.

Don't Empathize Too Much

Empathy and understanding are important, but there's a tendency these days to read too much into the bad behavior of kids. Sometimes that's all it is—bad behavior—and it may need more discipline than empathy.

Sometimes we're afraid to discipline the unacceptable emotional tirades of kids today because we don't want to damage their self-esteem or disregard their developmental needs. We want to *understand*. Such an approach may be fine for psychologists, but rarely is that true for parents. Bad manners, hateful remarks, and vile gestures are simply that and don't need to be interpreted any further. Grandpa probably had the right idea when he went for the hickory switch instead of the psychology book. While we may use appropriate logical consequences rather than physical punishment, the results are the same. Kids have to learn that certain behaviors (including verbal abuse) are not permitted under any circumstances.

Young people need to experience at home the kinds of standards and values they can expect to face in the real world. When they get a job someday, their boss isn't going to try to empathize with their emotions or try to understand their motivations. Either they do the job properly, or they'll be fired.

Actions Speak Louder Than Attitudes

There are things you may not like to do—in fact, may *loathe* doing—but chances are you do them anyway. That's what being an adult is all about.

It's unreasonable, therefore, to expect kids to do what you tell them to do with a good attitude. If a teenager is required to do something they don't want to do, they aren't going to like it. There's nothing wrong with that. If they grumble under their breath, scowl disgustedly, display rebellious body language, or act like they are being persecuted, no problem . . . as long as they aren't being disobedient. Don't be insulted or offended by a kid's bad attitude. In fact, you should expect it.

Your primary concern is behavior, not attitude. Remember that obedience with a bad attitude is always better than disobedience.

A bad attitude is perfectly understandable when someone isn't getting his way. If your teenager wants to stay out with his friends until three o'clock in the morning, and you (being the good parent you are) won't let him, then he's likely to feel ticked off about it. He'll have a bad attitude, which is perfectly okay, as long as he comes home at a reasonable hour.

There's no point in harping on the bad attitude of a teenager. It's better to just say, "Despite the fact you feel the way you do, I still expect you to obey." If your teenager grumbles while doing chores or obeying your direct instructions, fine. "You don't have to like it—just do it." Everybody gets stuck doing things they don't really feel like doing. But when they do, that shows maturity and responsibility. We want our teenagers to learn that. You don't have to feel right to do right.

If you insist on obedience with a good attitude, then you probably will get little obedience with a really bad attitude. But if you can handle obedience with a bad attitude, you'll more than likely get more obedience and, eventually (maybe), a better attitude to go with it.

Pick Your Battles Wisely

There's no good reason to jeopardize the relationship you have with your teenager over issues that have no lasting moral consequences.

After a stressful day at the office, Harold Iversen looked forward to a quiet evening at home. After battling forty-five minutes of rush-hour traffic, he pulled into the driveway of his home, swerving to barely miss his son's skateboard lying in the path of his car. *Is that the same $200 skateboard Jeremy wanted so badly for his birthday this year?* As he walked toward the house, he noticed that the front lawn was still badly in need of mowing, despite the fact that he had asked Jeremy to cut it several days ago. He made his way to the front porch only to notice a football in the flower bed next to several crushed chrysanthemums that had been annihilated by the incoming missile. He entered the house, not bothering to open the front door because *somebody* had left it wide open—with the air conditioning going full blast. The fresh muddy footprints on the entryway carpet revealed the culprit.

Harold angrily stomped into the kitchen, tripped over a backpack full of books left in the middle of the floor, and found the remains of Jeremy's afternoon snack on the kitchen table. With his blood pressure increasing with each step, he marched upstairs to confront his son with his transgressions.

His aching head throbbed with the vibration of rock music coming through the walls. He flung open Jeremy's bedroom door and was almost knocked out by the stench of smelly socks, gym clothes, stale junk food, and a grossly polluted fish aquarium. There, behind a pile of dirty laundry, CD cases, soda-pop cans, assorted sports paraphernalia, computer carcasses, and other debris, sat his teenage son wearing baggy shorts, a T-shirt advertising a bizarre rock group, and a head of bleached hair. Jeremy turned to his father and innocently grinned.

"Hi, Dad, what's up?"

◆ ◆ ◆

One thing I learned after I became the parent of a teenager is that it's possible to be ticked off twenty-four hours a day. There's *always* something you can be angry about.

Poor Harold Iversen stands in the doorway of his son's room with a real dilemma on his hands. He's angry and upset, his head is splitting, he's on the verge of serious child abuse, and his teenage son seems oblivious to it all. Now what is he supposed to do?

While this is an age-old problem for parents—knowing how to respond to

the relentlessly exasperating behavior of teenage children—it's as difficult to solve as ever. It's so easy to overreact or overdiscipline, to say hurtful or cruel things. So many families with teenagers are characterized by constant anger, conflict, and fighting. But nobody likes to live in a war zone.

Go Ballistic for the Right Reasons

Do you make a federal case out of your kids' failure to hang up their clothes or stack them neatly in their dresser? Do you blow a gasket when your teen fails to turn the lights off, uses all the hot water during a lengthy morning shower, or puts the empty milk carton in the refrigerator rather than the trash?

Interesting. As I write this paragraph, I'm trying to remember more examples of those things that really got to me when my three kids were home. I know they happened every day. But now that they are grown and no longer around to do them, I can't remember what they were. That probably says a lot about how "significant" they were in the grand scheme of things.

Most of the irritating, annoying things that teenagers do are simply that—irritating and annoying. Rarely are they serious enough to justify doing battle with your kids. They may indeed require some discipline and correction, but the situation probably does not warrant a declaration of war. Few indiscretions of teenagers are worth the anger and hostility they provoke on the part of parents.

Believe me, I understand completely how hard it is to keep from going ballistic when your kid belches at the dinner table or leaves one of your good tools out in the rain. But I think one of the reasons we go to war on these things is because we know we can win. But just as in a real war, winning can leave behind a good deal of collateral damage.

Worth the Sweat

It's true that you shouldn't sweat the small stuff, but it's not true that all stuff is small. Some stuff is definitely worth sweating, worth going to battle over.

I can't tell you exactly where to draw your battle lines, but I can tell you that with my own teenagers I tried to skirmish only over behavior that would likely result in serious moral, ethical, or physical consequences. Such a guideline eliminates most youthful behavior from consideration and separates the serious from the merely annoying.

Every parent should be willing to do whatever it takes to impress upon their kids that lying, cheating, stealing, using drugs or alcohol, reckless driving, sexual promiscuity, and vandalism are forbidden and will not be allowed under any circumstances.

Are other issues worth battling? Perhaps. But remember—nobody dies when your kids don't clean their rooms, lift toilet seats, or wear makeup in moderation. There's no good reason to jeopardize the relationship you have with your kids over issues that have no lasting moral consequences. Serious issues will undoubtedly arise, requiring you to be tough and uncompromising. When they do, you will want to win decisively. The best strategy therefore is to save your big guns for those crucial confrontations.

The relationship you have with your teenager is just as important as the discipline and guidance you provide. You can and must put that relationship at risk for the greater good of proper discipline, but there's no payoff at all in sacrificing it over the small stuff. If you are tough on the tough issues, your kids will come to respect and appreciate you even though they may not act like it at the time. Your relationship will survive and eventually thrive.

29

Put a Sock in It

Parents who have established their authority don't have to argue with their teenagers.

Dylan, the lawn needs mowing."

"I mowed it a week ago. It doesn't need to be mowed again. Besides, I'm tired."

"Dylan, you know it's your responsibility to mow the lawn by Saturday every week."

"Well the lawn looks fine to me."

"We have company coming tomorrow and it doesn't look fine, so get out there now and mow the lawn."

"If you want it done so much, why don't you do it yourself? I'm not the only one who knows how to mow the lawn!"

"Dylan, I've about had it with your back talk! I can't believe I'm raising such a lazy good-for-nothing. You just lay around all day listening to that jungle music of yours, and you can't even do a simple thing like mow the lawn once a week."

"That's not fair, Dad. I do stuff. I'd do a lot more if you weren't always yelling at me."

"I yell at you because you don't do anything! I can't believe you're so lazy. What are you going to do when you're older? Do you think you're always going to find somebody else to wait on you hand and foot? I pity your future wife, I really do. So help me, Dylan, you had better straighten yourself out real soon."

"I'm not lazy. I just don't want to mow the lawn right now."

"Honestly, do you know how hard I work to support this family? You have no idea what it takes to earn a living and keep clothes on your back and food on the table."

"I'm getting out of here. Mow your own stupid lawn!"

"Dylan, don't you dare talk to me like that. You come back in here!"

The mistakes being made by the father in this dialogue are almost too numerous to mention. But chief among them is that the argument ever took place at all. Wise parents never *ever* argue with their teenagers.

Do you find yourself arguing with your teenager frequently? Most parents who admit that they do will say it is because they have an argumentative or strong-willed child. But in reality, that is not the case. Parents who have established their authority don't have to argue with their teenagers, even those who are argumentative or strong-willed. If parents are unwilling to argue, there can be no argument. Parents have the power to end all arguments immediately.

In other words, save your breath. Put a sock in it. It does no good whatsoever to argue with a teenager. Parent-teen arguments are almost always counterproductive, and rather than reinforcing your authority, they erode it.

Walk Away

Dylan's father should have ended the argument right after his son's first response to his request to mow the lawn by saying, "You know, Dylan, if I were you, I might feel the same way. But you still need to mow the lawn. Now whether you do or not is entirely up to you."

Then he should have walked away. Nothing else needed to be said. The ball (or the lawn mower in this case) would have been squarely in Dylan's court. Dylan might have protested some more, but his protests would have gone unheeded. Eventually he would be left with the decision to mow the lawn or to disobey and suffer the consequences. And if Dylan's father had structured his relationship with his son correctly, there would most certainly have been consequences.

Would the lawn have been mowed? Maybe—maybe not. But by walking away, the chances would have increased, not decreased.

Most arguments we have with teenagers are nothing more than power struggles. Teenagers throw down the gauntlet, and parents rush to pick it right up. Teens have nothing to lose, so they push the confrontation to the limit. Meanwhile parents are forced to enter into a struggle they can't win. The more parents protest, lecture, and threaten, the more their authority is being diminished.

You really can't reason with an angry teenager. There is nothing in the world that parents can say in a heated argument to persuade them to change their mind. If you offer an explanation, they will think it's stupid. If you demand respect, they'll know you're on the defensive and become even more rigid. If you threaten, they'll act like they don't care.

It's unlikely that any teenager in the history of the world has ever ended an argument with his or her parents by saying, "You know, you're right, Dad. I never thought of it that way before. I was wrong." Teenagers can't really be argued into understanding a parent's point of view. They will understand only when they themselves become parents and have teenage children who are arguing with them.

Remember, your objective as a parent is not to win arguments but to help your teenager learn to make good decisions and become responsible. By walking away from an argument, you force your son or daughter to think things over and make a decision on their own without your interference. You also want to give your teenager a chance to come out a winner, and the likelihood of that happening increases significantly when you avoid the power struggle.

Stay Calm

Arguing can be avoided with teenagers, but conflict cannot. Conflict is normal, and sometimes it's necessary.

Did you ever get mad at your parents when you were a teenager? I know I did. I can remember being so angry with my folks that I tried running away from home. I never got very far, and nobody ever missed me, but I did try. I couldn't wait to leave home, which probably means they did a good job of making me independent.

Sure, you want to stay close to your kids while they are teenagers, but you can't be so concerned about getting along with them that you fail to exercise discipline when it's necessary. Conflict and closeness are not opposites but two sides of the same coin. If you eliminate all the conflict, you also have to eliminate all the rules, the limits, and the discipline that is needed to raise healthy, self-reliant kids.

If it's any consolation, remember that when your teenager gets mad at you, this might mean you are doing the right thing. Kids generally don't like having limits placed on their freedom, and they may respond with weeping, wailing, and "gnashing of teeth." But they'll get over it and so will you.

When conflict does occur, be careful. It's easy to lose control. If you are competitive, you'll want to win. If you are sensitive, you'll feel pain. If you have a short fuse, you may go ballistic. Teenagers know which buttons to push, and they may try to draw you into an arena where they think they can win.

Don't take the bait. Stay calm and focused. And above all, don't use physical violence of any kind. When your son or daughter was little, you may have used spanking as a disciplinary measure, but teenagers experience spanking or hitting by a parent quite differently from children. In response to a blow, a teenager can become violently upset. The cardinal rule is—don't ever hit your teenager.

Just Wait

If you walk away from conflict feeling angry or discouraged, don't carry those negative emotions around for days or let them cripple you. Just as coaches tell their players to "leave it on the field," so you shouldn't let conflict with your kids ruin your life or your family's life. That only gives them additional power over you.

The best thing to do is go about your business and wait. If your kids were disobedient or disrespectful, they'll probably be in for quite a shock when you demonstrate you haven't forgotten what they did by strictly enforcing logical consequences. Exercising your authority will produce much better results than your anger.

If there were harsh words and hurt feelings, it may be appropriate to sit down and have a talk. Not all conflicts require debriefing, but some do. You may want to find a time when tempers have cooled to discuss the situation.

The objective is not to get in a last parting shot or to explain yourself better, to inform your teen about how much he or she hurt you, or to lecture your teen on principles of communication. Most of the time, such attempts to fix things will only make things worse.

It's good to sit down and talk with your kids after a time of conflict when you can do it in a less confrontational manner. There may be a real need for forgiveness, reconciliation, and healing that can only come from a time of confession, listening, affirmation, and prayer. Scripture teaches that we shouldn't let the sun go down while we are still angry (Ephesians 4:26).

I can remember several times when Marci and I found it necessary to sit down with our kids to clear the air. Things had been building up, harsh words had left someone hurting, or a problem continued to repeat itself. By taking the time to talk in an honest and open way with our kids, we entered into a deeper relationship with them. The conflict actually gave us an opportunity to pay attention to some needy aspect of our relationship. We were able to listen to each other and make new commitments to love each other better.

If your kids know what is expected of them and know the consequences of misbehavior or disobedience, you don't have to say a thing. Actions always speak louder than words.

30

Don't Require Them
to Misbehave

Watch me! Watch me!

L ittle children love it when parents pay attention to what they are doing. Sadly, children do eventually stop the *watch mes*, but they never stop wanting attention and approval from their parents. Have you ever watched a football game on television and observed three-hundred-pound linemen turn to the camera, grin, and say "Hi, Mom!" They're still performing for the only audience who really counts—Mom and Dad.

Teenagers are no different. They thrive on attention from their parents. If they can't get it one way, they'll try to get it another way. If they can't get affirmation, they'll take admonishment. Either way, they just don't want to be ignored.

That's why some kids seem to enjoy being in constant trouble. They misbehave because it's the only way they can get their parents to notice them. Like hypochondriacs who stay sick because of all the attention they get from well-wishers and caregivers, some kids thrive on being the center of attention, the reason for everyone's concern.

The Power of Affirmation

In the same way, kids who get an abundance of praise and affirmation for positive behavior will be more likely to repeat it. Affirmation truly is a powerful motivator that not only encourages positive behavior but also builds self-esteem. Many teenagers unfortunately get very little of it from parents or anyone else. One researcher has claimed that every day the average teenager hears nine negative or critical remarks for every one that is positive or complimentary. I'm not sure most kids even get that one.

One of the best ways to raise healthy, self-reliant kids is to catch them in the act of doing something good as often as you can. This sounds easy, but it's not. It takes considerable effort to remember to notice and reward positive behavior. As parents, we sometimes tend to think that good behavior is expected and shouldn't require praise. But what seems obvious to us rarely is for kids. If they don't get affirmation from someone for what they do, they are unlikely to do it. There's not much in the way of a payoff.

I'll always be grateful to my parents for being a wonderful audience to play to as a kid. They were my biggest fans. They not only gave me affirmation when I did well, but they were constantly bragging about me to everyone they knew. Looking back, I realize now what a gift that was to me. I wasn't exceptionally talented or smart or well-behaved, but they sure did make me feel special.

Did they get on my case when I messed up? Absolutely. Their discipline was swift and unambiguous, but they didn't blow my indiscretions out of proportion or make me feel like a complete failure. None of my mess-ups were able to reduce the amount of self-esteem they had deposited into my emotional bank account.

One of the fondest memories I have of my father is how much he enjoyed my jokes. He would howl with laughter at the dumbest jokes that I would tell at the dinner table. I never realized the significance of that until my own kids became teenagers and started telling jokes at the dinner table. They aren't very funny. It's hard to laugh at your kids' jokes! But my dad laughed at mine, God bless him, and as a result I became pretty good at telling funny stories. And believe me, that has been a valuable asset to me as a public speaker and youth worker.

Praise Pointers

Perhaps you are a positive person by nature and praising comes easily for you. But for the majority of us, we have to be intentional about it and work

at it. I for one have found it helpful to remember the following points and to put them into practice regularly:

1. *Be there.* Unless you are there to notice the good they do, you won't be able to affirm it. Spend plenty of time with your kids. Go to their activities, games, and performances, giving them the unmistakable support of your presence. I know this is tough for today's busy parents, but kids don't understand why a business meeting or a prior engagement can be more important than they are.

2. *Practice the vocabulary of love.* I've heard parents comment, "I really don't know how to communicate to my teenager how much I love him." Actually, the best way is to use words. Just say nice things to your kids once in a while. Say "please" and "thank you" and "I love you" and "I'm

proud of you." Don't assume your kids know you love them. Tell her to her face and she'll get the message.

3. *Be specific.* Affirmation is always most effective when you look for specific behaviors to praise. For example, it's better to say, "Thanks for helping bring in the groceries," than "You've been a good kid today." Being a good kid is certainly positive, but does that mean he's not a good kid if he doesn't help with the groceries?

4. *Look for qualities of character you can praise.* If you notice your teen being particularly helpful or courteous or courageous or inventive, mention it. Praising character traits (the things that are on the inside) are worth more than flattery (things that are on the outside).

5. *Don't worry about the response.* Sometimes we wish kids would say "thank you," "you're welcome," or "Gosh, Dad, I really appreciate those words of encouragement." Forget it. Kids don't know how to respond, but that doesn't mean they don't want the affirmation. Keep doing it anyway.

6. *Praise progress, not perfection.* Sometimes we withhold praise because they didn't get it *exactly* right. Teenagers rarely do. They usually can't do anything as well as their parents, and their parents—being the perfectionists they are—refuse to give them their approval until they do. Look for small steps in the right direction, attempts to do well, even if they don't get it perfect.

7. *Avoid flattery.* Be sincere when you praise. Don't invent compliments just so you can say something positive to your kids. If you tell your daughter, "You are definitely the smartest girl in the school," she won't believe it because she knows it isn't true (even if you think it is). If you tell your son, "You played a great game today," when, in fact, he played poorly, he'll know you aren't shooting straight with him. It's better to be honest, yet positive.

8. *Praise publicly.* Even though kids will sometimes act shy and pretend they are embarrassed by public praise, deep down they love it when parents brag on them to friends or extended family. We can show our pride in them by displaying their artwork, showing off newspaper clippings, inviting them to perform on a musical instrument, reading to guests something they have written. Putting pictures of them on your

desk at the office or on your Web page or even on the refrigerator door will demonstrate publicly how thankful you are for your kids, and it will acknowledge how well they are doing. When kids know that they have a reputation outside the home to live up to, they just might do it!

According to Scripture, "As he thinks in his heart, so is he" (Proverbs 23:7, NKJV). If you let your kids know that you are proud of them and that you believe in them, there's a strong chance that they'll start to believe in themselves too.

Lighten Up

When a youngster turns thirteen, put him in a pickle barrel, nail the lid shut and feed him through a knothole. Then, when he turns sixteen, plug up the knothole.

—Mark Twain

Twain's famous joke about teenagers still makes me chuckle. But some parents of teenagers aren't laughing much—not because they don't get the joke, but because they've lost their sense of humor. Hopefully you haven't gotten to the point where you can't laugh a little bit about having teenagers in your house. It's likely that someday you'll reflect on a lot of what you're going through right now and laugh about it. Why not laugh now?

Nothing turns a teenager off faster than adults who have no sense of humor. That's why successful youth ministers generally are such fun-loving people who don't mind acting silly and looking stupid from time to time. Kids can relate to them. Granted, youthful humor can sometimes be a little bizarre, but it's still humorous to them. The challenge for adults who want to treat kids respectfully is to learn to laugh with them. This is just as true for parents as it is with youth workers and teachers.

> You know your kids are growing up when they stop asking you where they came from and stop telling you where they're going.

It's often overlooked in the psychological literature on parenting, but there's no doubt that healthy families are usually characterized by an abundance of laughter. Show me a home full of people who have fun together

137

and who can laugh out loud together, and I'll show you a healthy home. There's absolutely no denying it.

Granted, this suggests one of those "chicken-egg" questions—"Which came first, the healthy home or the laughter?" Why wait to find out? Start laughing now. Have fun with your kids. Lighten up! Psychologist David Elkind in his book *All Grown Up and No Place to Go* writes that "without exception, parents who succeed with their teenagers have a special sense of humor . . . they can balance the headaches that teenagers provoke against the pleasures of their unique charm and creativity." Having teenagers around the house really can be a lot of fun. They can lift your spirits even when they are wearing you down. Sometimes the secret to parenting is finding that balance.

> I'm worried about my kids' eyesight. My daughter can't find anything to wear in a closet full of clothes, and my son can't find anything to eat in a refrigerator full of food.

Notify Your Face

One of the best gifts you can give your teenager is a smile. In the workplace, you know the importance and value of greeting people with a smile and letting them know that you are glad to see them. That's just being courteous and respectful. Sometimes we forget to do this when we are at home.

What message do you nonverbally communicate to your kids when they get home from school, come to the dinner table, or when they finally emerge from their bedroom after sleeping until noon on Saturday? I know you may still be upset because they didn't do their chores, left dirty laundry in the bathroom floor, or broke curfew last night, which resulted in some harsh words. But even if there's some unfinished business to take care of later, you can still be pleasant, can't you? What your kids need to know is that you still love them and are happy to see them, even when there are problems. Let's face it, there will always be problems. But the time you have with your kids is short.

> Sound travels slowly when your kids are teenagers. What you tell them today won't reach their ears until they are in their forties.

Sound travels slowly when your kids are teenagers. What you tell them today won't reach their ears until they are in their forties.

Be Silly

I have a friend who somehow acquired a realistic-looking gorilla outfit. He put it on early one morning and sneaked into his kids' bedrooms, scaring them half to death while his wife captured it all on videotape. Even though the kids eventually needed therapy to deal with their recurring gorilla nightmares (just kidding), they sure had fun watching those videos later on.

When our three kids were still at home, my wife suggested that we all go to a thrift store, buy some goofy-looking clothes, and dress up like a family of nerds. While the kids weren't too thrilled with the idea at first, we coaxed them into the car after dinner and did some shopping. I found a silly-looking toupee that didn't match my hair, a leisure suit coat with plaid pants, a bow tie, and a loud shirt. My wife found the ugliest dress in the universe, put her hair up in a bun, and rolled her nylons down around her ankles. The kids also found silly clothes, glasses, plastic pocket protectors, and other nerd accessories like an accordion and a pair of earmuffs. Once we were all dressed up in our outfits, we had a family portrait taken, which we enclosed in our Christmas cards that year. Everyone who got one of those pictures had a good laugh, and so did we. Even though we all looked and felt pretty foolish at the time, our kids enjoyed knowing (and letting others know) that they were part of a fun-loving family.

> One of the first signs of maturity in a teenager is when they discover that the volume control knob also turns to the left.

What is your family identity? Are you fun for your kids to be around? Can members of your family play practical jokes on each other without someone taking it too personally? Do you look forward to an evening of Pictionary or Taboo or some other fun game that generates laughter and healthy interaction? Are you creating some memories for your kids that might have a positive impact on their own families someday?

If laughter comes easily for your family, then getting through tough times will come a lot easier also. Wise parents aren't afraid to let their hair down once in a while and have fun with their kids whenever they can.

Joy in the Journey

It was the apostle Paul who said, "Rejoice in the Lord always. I will say it again: Rejoice!" (Philippians 4:4). Our kids are more likely to hear, "How could you be so stupid?! I say it again: What on earth were you thinking?!"

Certainly Paul had more than enough trials and tribulations for one person, yet he strongly urged people to be thankful, to keep a positive outlook, to rejoice no matter the circumstances. Parents also need to find joy in the journey—not only when the ride is smooth, but also when things get a little bumpy. So you've got a moody, belligerent teenager? You just got his report card with one too many Fs on it? You're having a bad hair day because you couldn't get into the bathroom thanks to your preening teenage daughter (or son)? You got in your car this morning and found the radio tuned to K-RAP 95 at full blast, french fries all over the floor, a sticky steering wheel, and a gas tank on empty? You have my sympathies. Nevertheless, "Rejoice in the Lord always. I will say it again: Rejoice!"

> Insanity is hereditary; you get it from your kids.

Paul went on to say, "Finally, brothers, whatever is true, whatever is noble, whatever is right, whatever is pure, whatever is lovely, whatever is admirable— if anything is excellent or praiseworthy—think about such things" (Philippians 4:8). In other words, try to focus on the positive. True, your kids will make their share of mistakes, and they will cause you to experience new negative emotions. But relax. Take a deep breath. Insulate your hot buttons and smile. The more problems you dwell on, the more problems you will have.

In family life, there's simply no substitute for parents who truly, honestly enjoy their kids. Teenagers need people around them who like them for who they are right now, not just for who they may someday become.

Help Them Harness Their Hormones

Talk with your teenagers as you would talk to any other adult about the subject of sex.

I'll never forget Maria, the pretty seventh-grader who boldly reached out and took my hand on the school bus one day. Besides giving me a very sweaty hand, she turned my whole world upside down. Sure I had *girlfriends* before then, but there had never been any physical contact—just some note passing and maybe sitting together at church or school activities. But when Maria took my hand, she escorted me into a whole new world of sexual feelings that were exciting and very new to me. Even though holding hands was all we did, I lost my "virginity" that day. I suddenly got very interested in sex.

Sounds like something out of the dark ages, doesn't it? Today it's not uncommon for junior highers to lose their virginity by having oral sex rather than holding hands. The cat's out of the bag. Our kids are exposed every day to messages that encourage them to have sex as soon as possible. The taboos have been lifted. The rules have changed. Sex is now a primary form of entertainment. It is used to sell everything from automobiles to underarm deodorants. What kids hear about sex—from the media, from advertising, from school, from friends, even from the White House—is that everybody's doing it, and if you aren't, there is something seriously wrong with you.

To their credit, most young people are pretty good at sifting out truth from reality and showing remarkable restraint. But a growing percentage of kids today feel compelled to have sex "just to get it over with." Like smoking, drugs, alcohol, and other harmful activities, sex has become a rite of passage, a way to assert their independence and announce their adulthood. In fact, the word *adult* now is almost synonymous with sex. It no longer has to do with maturity or responsibility, but obscenity. Films and TV shows with adult themes are those that feature sex. Stores that sell adult products are pornography stores. It's no wonder kids want to have sex. Sex is what adults do.

Setting an Example

Like everything else, kids get their values and attitudes about sex first from their parents. And what they learn is more than what parents tell them. They learn by example.

That's why if you are in a two-parent family, you should let your kids see what a healthy marriage looks like. That doesn't mean putting your sexual relationship on display in front of your kids, of course, but it doesn't hurt them to see their parents being romantic or touching each other in loving, tender ways. It's okay for kids to know that Mom and Dad enjoy a sexual relationship. Kids need to know that marriage is where sex belongs, and that if they will wait until marriage, they will have something wonderful to anticipate.

And whether you are married or single, it's crucial that you keep all of your relationships with the opposite sex above reproach. Some single parents allow their dates to spend the night and then wonder why their children are promiscuous. Moms and dads who are unfaithful send a powerful message to their children about sexual behavior. *Never* bring pornography into your home. Don't watch any of those adult (there's that word again) cable channels or Internet sites. Your computer-savvy kids will likely discover that you did.

Sex Talk

Everybody's talking about sex, it seems, except for parents and teenagers. Some researchers say that while 80 percent of parents believe they are responsible for teaching their kids about sex, only about 30 percent ever actually have conversations with their kids about it.

I know it's tough. Kids will squirm, look disinterested, act like they already know everything, or try to disappear as soon as you bring up the topic. It's no easier for parents. It's never comfortable talking about sex with your kids.

But you can't let that get in the way. Break the silence before it breaks your family. Talk about sex with your kids as openly and honestly as you can. Keep the communication lines open and make sure your kids know that it is not a prohibited subject around your house.

Actually, the best way to communicate openly about sex is by taking advantage of teachable moments. When the subject comes up (and it will quite frequently), use those times to share your thoughts and ask for theirs. An evening of prime-time TV is usually about all you need to get a pretty good discussion going.

Avoid lecturing. Sometimes kids think their parents talk about sex only because they don't trust them. That's why it's best to start early, before kids become teenagers. When you wait until they are sexually mature, kids start wondering why you have suddenly become so interested in the subject. It must be because you are worried or suspicious.

Talk with your teenagers as you would talk to any other adult about the subject. Be nonjudgmental and respectful. Sometimes you can use humor to break the ice when talking about sex, but you should avoid telling your kids off-color jokes. Off-color humor sends mixed messages about sexuality and can be very threatening to kids who are trying to make sense of it all. They don't need their parents contributing to their confusion.

Tools for Tackling Temptation

It's possible for parents to offer their kids a little coaching on how to handle sexual situations. Kids won't admit that they need your advice, but don't fail to give it to them anyway. Remind them of what the Bible teaches about sexual behavior. Sometimes a relevant verse of Scripture is all that they need to motivate them to say no to temptation.

Moms can teach their daughters how to resist the advances of boys who are only interested in sex, what to say when they hear the line, "If you really love me, you'll have sex with me." Dads can also talk to their daughters about boys so that they hear it from both parents. Moms can talk to their sons. Straightforward information about sex, contrary to the beliefs of some, doesn't encourage kids to have sex, it equips them to postpone it. Kids generally experiment with sex because they lack information, not because they have it.

Some parents have found it helpful to establish a "dating covenant" with their kids in which their teens pledge abstinence until marriage as the parents pledge increased freedom and trust. A special ring or pendant can be worn by the teenager to serve as a reminder of this covenant. If something like this feels right for you and your teenager, then go for it. Anything you can do to communicate clearly to your kids the truth about this important issue in today's fuzzy world will be a plus.

Set Limits

As with curfew, you have the right and the responsibility to impose and enforce rules concerning at what age they may start dating, who they date, where they go, and how long they stay out. Such rules will of course vary depending on age, maturity level, and past conduct, but you need to make sure your teenager knows what is allowed and what is not. No teenager likes rules, but in many cases they will appreciate having them in place when a difficult situation arises. For example, if your daughter is invited to a boy's house when parents are absent, it's a lot easier to say, "My parents won't allow me to be there" than to say, "I don't want to be there." They can say no and blame it on you. If you don't set some limits on your kids dating relationships, you are giving them permission to be promiscuous.

Remember that most kids who have sex do it in their homes or the homes of friends, usually after school or at other times when parents are absent. If you aren't home, don't allow your kids to invite friends over. If your kids go to parties or other social events with groups of kids, make sure they are well supervised. Obviously if kids want to have sex bad enough, they'll find a way regardless of how many rules you impose. But if you don't have any rules at all, you send a message to your kids that you don't really care what they do.

The Power of Touch

Touch is one of the important ways people express intimacy and closeness. Much has been said and written about "tough love" for parents, but not much about "touch love." Only one letter in one word differentiates the phrases, but they are miles apart in meaning.

Most kids engage in premature sexual activity not for physical reasons (raging hormones) but psychological ones. David Elkind in *Parenting Your Teenager* writes, "If teenagers feel secure, loved and appreciated at home, they are not likely to seek comfort and support elsewhere in the form of premature sexual intimacy." Kids who feel distant and disconnected from their parents will look for love and affection outside the home, often in a sexual relationship.

Touch is one of the ways parents can communicate love nonverbally to their children. Touching teenagers, however, is a lot different from touching younger kids. Teenagers have very ambivalent feelings about parental touch. They are aware of the sexual taboos regarding contact between parents and children. They don't appreciate condescending pats on the head or pinches on the cheek. Parental touch needs to be appropriate, respecting the teen's increased need for privacy and his or her growing sense of independence. The last thing you want to do is embarrass your teenager in a public place.

Still, it's important to touch your kids in natural, appropriate, nonsexual ways. It can sometimes be a hug, a welcoming embrace, or a hand on the shoulder. Holding hands at the dinner table while saying grace can be a meaningful gesture of love and solidarity. Even a wrestling match on the living-room floor communicates closeness and acceptance. Especially after a difficult time of conflict, touch can be wonderfully healing and affirming. Touch lets someone know that they are not "untouchable," that they are loved and accepted as they are.

Touch your kids, or somebody else will.

Wean Them off
Your Wallet

Our goal is to teach our teens to be good stewards, not good spenders.

Ever get tired of doling out money to your kids?
Well, if you teach your kids to manage their own money, you can dole no more.

This is a very important issue. It's no secret that kids today have a lot more money to manage than previous generations, and more advertisers than ever before target them. If you find today's TV commercials hard to understand, irreverent, and loud, that's because you aren't the audience the advertiser wants. They want your kids. Madison Avenue is well aware that the youth market is huge—and they know that if they can win a customer when they are thirteen or fourteen, they have a customer for life. Ask the tobacco industry.

According to researchers, the nation's 20 million teens spent over $141 billion in 1998. The average teenager spends about $84 per week, and a growing percentage of kids now have their own credit cards. Teens had a combined income of $121 billion in 1998, an increase of almost 10 percent over the previous year. Most of that income (57 percent) is given to them by parents in the form of an allowance or on an as-needed basis. The rest comes from part-time or full-time jobs. Besides what teens spend on themselves, they also influence many purchases made by their parents. It's not surprising that teens are a primary target for the advertising industry. This is a market to be taken seriously.

What do kids spend their money on? Not surprisingly, most of it is for CDs and videos, electronic equipment, computers and computer games, entertainment, makeup, jewelry, fad apparel, personal accessories, recreation, and all those other amenities of life that kids seem to find essential these days. It's no wonder that many young adults return home to live with their parents simply because they can't bear having to lower their standard of living by paying for their own housing, groceries, utilities, and taxes. When kids do gain their independence, if they don't know how to pay for it, they'll be back in a flash.

You can help your kids develop a healthy attitude toward money and learn to be responsible for it. Financial competence takes years to achieve, but practice and guidance under a parent's experienced eye may help kids learn the realities of living within your means.

Talk about Money; Don't Just Argue about It

Money is like sex—it's one of those personal things that people prefer to keep private. Some kids grow up with completely unrealistic ideas about money and where it comes from. Every time you go to the ATM machine and withdraw a handful of twenty-dollar bills, your observant kids may learn that money comes from a machine. Just stick your card in there and presto, instant money. What they want to know is, "Where do I get one of those cards?"

Teach your kids the financial facts of life. You can start by being honest with them about money, including yours. It's okay for them to know about your family's finances. Some kids have no idea what it costs to live in a house, buy groceries, and pay for utilities, insurance, taxes, automobiles, and everyday expenses. Some teenagers help out with the family finances by writing checks at bill-paying time or balancing the family's checkbook on the computer. Especially when finances are tight, kids can develop a better appreciation for the importance of staying on a budget and spending less than you earn.

Provide Your Teenager with an Income

Call it an allowance if you must, but give your kids a portion of the family income to manage on their own. How much is entirely up to you—but it should be enough to fund their personal financial needs such as recreation, discretionary clothing, entertainment, eating out, and other miscellaneous expenses they might have. If you do some honest accounting, you'll probably find that the amount you dole out for this kind of spending is substantial.

Once you have decided on a reasonable amount, give it to your son or daughter on a monthly rather than a weekly basis (one payday a month), and make it absolutely clear that no more money will be given to them for the rest of the month. It's up to them to make it last. You may want to agree to adjust the amount for inflation every year, but it's best not to promise a raise. As your kids get older, let them supplement their income on their own by doing odd jobs or finding other ways to earn money rather than getting more money from you.

Let Them Do the Shopping

Do you ever get into endless arguments with your kids over what they can or cannot buy? You are convinced that the sixty-dollar pair of athletic shoes that you found on sale look fine, but they insist that they can't live without those really cool $150 ones worn by the stars of WrestleMania. Just stay out of it. Let them learn to prioritize their spending by giving them a fixed amount of money each month and letting them decide how to spend it. It may take dozens of foolish decisions before they learn, but they *will* learn.

For younger teens especially, you can coach them by requiring that they do some research first. To discourage impulse buying, make them go to three different stores and compare prices on the items they want to buy. After they shop, insist that they wait a week before actually making the purchase to give them time to think it over and decide whether or not it is still a priority for them. These are good habits to develop.

My wife and I usually gave our kids extra money at the end of the summer for buying school clothes. We would first discuss with them what they really needed in the way of shoes, new outfits, and gym clothes, and then we gave them an appropriate amount of money to handle it all. If they could save money on some items, they would have enough to pay for those designer labels they coveted. It was entirely up to them, and they had to live with their decisions. Our daughter developed a remarkable fondness for shopping at thrift stores. She discovered that she could find some real bargains there and have money left over. The best part is that we never had to say a word. She figured this out on her own—the best way to learn anything.

Should you place limits on what kids can spend money on? The answer is yes, but don't expect or require your kids to spend money the way you would. You aren't going to like how they spend their money. Some obvious restrictions that you could place on their spending might include the purchase of anything that is harmful or dangerous (motorcycles, drugs, alcohol, guns) or anything that violates your family's moral code (like pornography or satanic paraphernalia). Set some limits, but coach their consumption rather than try to control it.

Get Them a Bank Account

You may be thinking "How can I expect my kid to manage a checking account when mine is overdrawn half the time?" Good point. But your kids are probably capable of learning the basics of banking when they are in high school. Let them open their own accounts (checking and savings), make deposits, write checks, get an ATM card, and balance their bank statements. They should learn how to manage a checking account, save money, and earn some interest at a bank or in a money-market account.

Teach Them about Credit

Sooner or later, your kids will make the discovery that it's possible to buy stuff today and pay for it tomorrow. *Is that cool or what?* Unfortunately, that discovery can be as addictive and ruinous as drugs. That's why it's important to help kids learn how credit works and how it can be used properly. Credit is beneficial when used wisely, but it can also do a lot of damage.

One simple way to teach your kids about credit is to make them loans rather than giving them additional money when emergencies come up. If your teenager loses his jacket, for example, he may need to buy a new one. You may feel sorry for him (that's okay), but he needs to learn to be responsible for taking care of his things. Rather than being an insurance company and replacing the jacket, it's better to be a bank and extend him a loan, with interest that he must pay back in regular monthly installments. You can even do a "credit check" verifying that he is able to handle the new obligation. If he doesn't make the payments, repossess the jacket.

In all likelihood, your teen will start receiving offers from credit-card companies while they are still in high school. Our cashless society (and the increase in Internet shopping) practically requires that you have a credit-card account today. But hardly anything is more hazardous to a person's financial health. Millions of people who declare bankruptcy every year quickly find out that credit-card debt can cripple a person for years.

Even if your teenager doesn't have their own credit-card account, teach them how to use one properly. Let them use one of yours, and set up a "sub-account" for them that you manage. Insist that they not spend more money than they have and that they pay off their credit-card balance in full every month. They need to learn as soon as possible that credit-card interest is a huge waste of money and will often plunge them into serious financial trouble. Of course the best way to teach this is to model it yourself. If you can show your kids your own credit-card statements that reflect responsible credit habits, you'll add real credibility to your teaching.

Teach Kids to Give

An important part of instilling fiscal responsibility in kids is to teach them to be unselfish with what they have. All we have comes from God (James 1:17), and we should be gratefully willing to give a portion of it back to Him to benefit others. Jesus taught "Give, and it will be given to you" (Luke 6:38), a principle that has stood the test of time. Generous people are blessed people, and kids need to learn that giving is their duty and privilege before God. Some parents make tithing a requirement for their kids, but I don't believe this is the best way to teach it. It's best to model generosity in front of children and to let them know that giving to God and to others is a family priority.

Encourage your kids to give to their church, to a youth ministry that has touched their lives, or to some other organization at home or abroad. Many teenagers sponsor underprivileged children through mission agencies like Compassion International and learn at an early age that a few dollars can make a big difference in the lives of others.

Teach Them the Real Value of Money

There's no question that our kids are growing up in a material world. Money is the false god most people serve today. As Christian parents, we need to communicate clearly and often to our kids that money cannot buy love, happiness, health, or anything that is truly important in life. While it is worthwhile for kids to learn how to be responsible for what money they do have, they also need to learn that money is not necessary for them to live well. With few exceptions, money actually has an inverse relationship to happiness. The truly happy are rarely ever the rich.

By your example, you can help your kids develop an attitude of gratitude for what they have. If they are faithful with the little that God has given them, they can expect that God will bless them with even more (Luke 16:10). Remember: Our goal is to teach our kids to be good stewards, not good spenders.

Monitor the Monitors
in Your Home

Times sure have changed. When I was a kid, I remember coming home from school, getting a snack, and turning on the TV. My son comes home from school, gets his snack, and turns on the computer to check his e-mail.

I f you were born in the fifties or sixties, you were among the first genera-tion to be raised on television. If your children were born in the eighties or nineties, they are among the first generation to be raised on computers.

It is estimated that 97 percent of American homes have TV sets. More than 70 percent also have personal computers. (And that percentage is on the rise.) Researchers say that Americans spend more than nine years of their lives watching television and another four in front of the computer (not including time at work if your job involves using a computer).

While both the television and the computer are marvelous inventions that provide families with an incredible array of entertainment options, informa-tion, and activity, they need to be controlled carefully by parents who want their kids to grow up as healthy adults.

Consider this: Every child is born with incredible potential for develop-ment in every area of life—intellectual, artistic, musical, athletic, inter-personal, and spiritual. During their formative years—especially early child-hood and early adolescence—their potential is stimulated by exposure to environments and experiences that provide opportunities for exploration, discovery, imaginative play, and social interaction. Kids don't get those things when they are sitting in front of a TV or computer screen. Instead, they are being robbed of precious time they need to develop their God-given capabilities and competencies.

TV—the Plug-in Drug

TV critics abound, but most focus on the *content* of TV—the idiotic programs, the advertising, the foul language, sex, and violence. While there's no denying that TV programming is a wasteland, that's not its real danger. The problem with TV is that it is a colossal waste of time.

Kids learn best by doing things; everybody knows that. But what do kids do when they watch TV? The answer is *absolutely nothing*. Not one skill or talent is being developed by watching television.

Rather than helping kids learn and grow, TV actually inhibits the development of initiative, curiosity, resourcefulness, creativity, motivation, imagination, reasoning, problem-solving abilities, communication skills, social skills, fine motor skills, eye-hand coordination, and attention span. It inhibits these skills because they can only be developed by experience, by doing something.

TV is at least partially to blame for our kids' lower scholastic achievement test scores. As a nation, our literacy level has steadily declined since 1955, when children started watching television. Today, one of every five seventeen-year-olds in this country is functionally illiterate. Since the 1950s, learning disabilities have become epidemic in our schools, both public and private. Learning-disabled kids usually have problems with their visual-scanning abilities. They can't smoothly scan a line of print from left to right. They also have less eye-hand coordination and fine and gross motor skills. They can't read very well. They have problems with active-listening and communication skills. They lack problem-solving abilities and creativity. They tend to be passive and easily frustrated when problems confront them. They tend to be unimaginative and have short attention spans. In short, there's a direct parallel between the skills that television fails to provide and the symptoms of today's learning-disabled kids. It doesn't take a rocket scientist to figure out why millions of today's kids are diagnosed with ADD (attention deficit disorder).

TV also encourages a sedentary rather than an active lifestyle. One study of four hundred adolescent boys found that those who watched TV more than ten hours per week were significantly less physically fit than those who didn't. It's not surprising that we are the most overweight country on earth. We have become a nation of watchers who live life vicariously through the lives of celebrities and sports stars rather than living meaningful, active lives of our own.

And then there is, of course, the content of TV. Kids themselves report that what they see on TV encourages them to have sex too soon, be more aggressive, be more disrespectful to parents, and buy more stuff than they can afford. According to researchers, before your kids finish elementary school, they will see more than 100,000 acts of violence, 100,000 beer commercials, and 100,000 sex scenes.

But the real danger of TV's content is that none of it is real. It's all fantasy. Even educational or news programs are scripted and edited so that you see only what the producers want you to see. Kids need to be taught a healthy skepticism of what they see on TV.

Our goal as parents is to help our kids grow up and succeed in the real world. They won't learn to live in the real world by watching make-believe all day. Pushing a button on the remote control cannot change real life. That myth often takes years to unlearn.

Controlling It

You'll have more success controlling the TV than controlling your kids. Especially when they become teenagers, you shouldn't have to tell them what to watch or not watch. You won't be able to follow them around the rest of their lives. They need to learn to make their own choices. But you can set a good example for them and control the TV in your home.

Consider no TV. Just get rid of it. Believe it or not, some parents have done this successfully without a family mutiny. In most cases, kids just find other ways to occupy their time. I recommend this only if you don't think you can control the TV any other way.

Turn it off. If you have trouble keeping it off, try putting it on a timer so that it can't be turned on until a certain hour of the day. You'll be amazed at how creative kids (and maybe you yourself) can get when the TV isn't on.

Don't buy that second TV set, and for heaven's sake, don't put one in your kid's bedroom. Oops, too late? Then sell it or disconnect the antenna. Really, nothing is more damaging to family connectedness than everybody watching what they want to watch in their own private watching places. One TV in your family room is enough, preferably one of normal size rather than one of those giant screens (which tend to dominate everything else in the room). Then, when the TV is on, everybody can watch together after negotiating which shows will be watched. Set a good example for your kids and lose the TV in your own bedroom too.

Bring back the rabbit ears. Do you really watch all those channels? What more do you need beside four networks and PBS? Remember, less is more when it comes to TV.

Discourage or disallow weekday TV, or limit it to one hour per evening, after everything else is done—homework, chores, dinnertime, family time, whatever. On weekends and holidays, the TV can get more use, but it should never be left on when nobody's watching.

Insist that the TV only be turned on after deciding what to watch. Don't allow channel surfing. Check the TV listings, and make your family's TV time more intentional and purposeful. Use the VCR to tape-record desirable programs that can then be viewed at your family's convenience.

Go on a TV diet from time to time, maybe during the summer when there's nothing but reruns anyway. Or give it up for Lent. Whatever works for you. Just unplug it and leave it off. You'll be amazed at how easy it is to survive without TV for an extended period of time.

Talk over TV. When you *are* watching TV, talk about what you are watching. You're not in a movie theater, so you don't have to worry about an usher telling you to be quiet. Think out loud. That teaches your kids how to think when they watch TV.

What about the Computer?

Computers are so new it's difficult to assess their impact on kids and families. One thing we do know is that today's kids are computer savvy and use them daily, either at school or at home. Surfing the Web is now a primary leisure-time activity for teenagers, right up there with hanging out with friends.

Like TV, the computer has become a primary source of entertainment and information. But unlike the television set, it can transform itself into a shopping mall, a library, a post office, a stereo system, an art studio, or a movie theater. You have access to a museum, a swap meet, a bank, a travel agency, a telephone, a game room, a classroom, a file cabinet, a film processor, a checkbook, a discussion group, a stockbroker, a typewriter, an encyclopedia, or even a Bible. Or the computer can become an adult bookstore, a peep show, a cult recruiter, a bomb-making guide, a virtual sex encounter, or a place where pedophiles can say hello to your kids. Exciting, isn't it?

While kids benefit tremendously from learning to use a computer and navigating their way around cyberspace, there are some real concerns. As with TV, the biggest issue has to do with time. Today's computers may be faster than ever before, but they still consume huge blocks of time your kids could spend more productively elsewhere.

156

There also is the proliferation of Web sites dealing in pornography, racism, gambling, and the occult. If your kids spend any time at all on-line, there's a better than even chance they will stumble across some pretty disgusting Web sites.

Then there is the growing popularity of Internet chat rooms where nameless, faceless people interact with each other instantly. This has tremendous appeal for kids who like to try on different personalities. They can become anybody they want to be. Of course, so can perverts and pedophiles who pretend to be teenagers and strike up on-line relationships with your kids.

Despite the dangers, kids should be allowed and encouraged to learn all they can about computers. They will play a huge role in your children's future.

Get computer savvy yourself. The more you know about computers, the easier it will be to help your kids use a computer responsibly.

Limit computer time. As with TV, you can set limits on how much time your kids spend on the computer.

Keep it in plain view. As with TV sets, usually one per family is enough. Learn to share.

Consider a family-friendly Internet service provider like Net Nanny or Internet 4 Families that filters out objectionable content.

Or try a computer-monitoring software like WinGuardian which provides you with a record of every Web site visited on your computer, every program opened or closed, every keystroke made. Rather than restricting what kids can do on the computer, it just holds them accountable.

Fire the Chauffeur

If the state knew my teenager, the driving age would be raised to thirty-five.

Besides graduation from high school, there is hardly a more significant rite of passage than turning sixteen and becoming eligible for a driver's license. Besides the freedom and status that it represents, it's an official acknowledgment by the state of a person's adult status. On the highway, everybody's the same. This is an awesome responsibility that your teenager is absolutely, positively sure he or she can handle.

But if you are like most parents, you aren't so sure. Relax. While age is rarely the best way to determine a person's ability to do anything (let alone drive), your teenager will probably be capable of operating an automobile safely at the ripe old age of sixteen. Obviously he or she will need plenty of supervision, along with whatever classroom and on-the-job training is required, but there's a strong likelihood your teenager has the right stuff to be a good driver.

Teens are a greater accident risk due to their inexperience (duly noted by insurance companies), but as a group, teenagers are in no more danger than you and I are when we get behind the wheel of a car. We are told that death by auto accident is the number one killer of teens in America, but that's because teens are not as susceptible to death by cancer, heart disease, or other ailments that generally strike adults. According to National Highway Traffic Administration statistics, driving fatality rates among males in their

early twenties are actually higher than those involving teenagers. Teens do have a higher percentage of fender benders and other accidents that keep insurance rates high.

A driver's license is a major affirmation of a teen's emerging adulthood and independence, and it can also provide new opportunities for them to become more responsible. In exchange for the privilege of being able to drive the family car, your teen may need to take care of it, buy gas or insurance, keep it clean, and drive for other members of the family. Remember that our goal as parents is to help our kids become responsible adults.

Celebrate this important rite of passage in the life of your teenager rather than downplaying it. Unless your sixteen-year-old has failed to take responsibility for getting the driver education and training he needs, encourage him to make his appointment with the department of motor vehicles, get a good score on the driver test, smile for the camera, and start providing some of his or her own transportation. Make a big deal out it and *fire the chauffeur*.

Whose Car Do They Drive?

Most teenagers hope their parents will buy them a new car, preferably something fast and sporty-looking. After all, they've had nightmares about having to drive to school in plain view of their friends in the family station wagon or minivan.

But that's exactly what our kids drove to school, and they survived. Your main consideration should always be safety. You want something for your teenager that is not too small (no protection), not too big (hard to handle), not too fast (tickets), not too old (unreliable), and not too expensive (insurance!). A late-model mid-size sedan is probably ideal.

Your teen's or your family's economic situation will probably have a lot to do with what kind of car your teenager drives. The cost of a car, plus gas, insurance, and upkeep can be considerable, and you shouldn't feel obligated to go out on a financial limb just so your teenager can have wheels. Most teens can understand and accept those realities if you are honest with them: Sometimes they will want to get a job to help purchase their own car. If your son or daughter can hold down a job without his or her grades suffering or causing any other negative impact on the family, this might be an option. But having a car is not worth sacrificing their education.

We chose not to buy our kids their own cars because we didn't want them to become too independent too soon. When young people have their own cars, they start thinking parents have no jurisdiction over them at all. We decided that this was not a battle we wanted to fight. So we always had an extra car around that our kids could drive, but it belonged to us. We did, however, buy all three of our kids their own cars after they graduated from high school. Since they were going away to college, we wanted them to have reliable transportation.

Rules of the Road

Whether you buy your kids their own car or allow them to drive the family car, some rules should be in place. Here are a few suggestions:

1. Never go anywhere without telling us where you are going, how long you'll be gone, who you'll be with, and what you'll be doing. Not that

we're snoops, mind you, but you don't want us to worry.

2. We will provide the car, but you will pay for your own insurance, gas, and upkeep. (Some parents make the kids pay for all car expenses, but in our case, since our teen's driving was of great benefit to us, we were willing to pay for that. It also underscored our ownership of the car.)

3. If grades drop as a result of the additional responsibilities you are assuming, your driving privileges can and will be suspended. (Parents should be quite specific about this to avoid disputes later on. How much can grades drop? What does a suspension mean? How long will it last? Sometimes a probation period is established that only allows driving to school or to work until grades are improved.)

4. Traffic citations and accidents will also result in a suspension of driving privileges, depending on how serious they are. (Again, be as specific as possible. Try to allow some room here for grace and understanding on the parents' part. Most accidents are indeed "accidents" with natural consequences which teach them all they need to learn.)

Other Coaching Tips

When your kids start driving, you should set other limits, like the number of passengers they can carry. During the first few weeks, you might want to make that number zero and work up from there. The chances of an accident increase with more people in the car, as well as the risk of injury to passengers. Kids don't drive the same way alone as they do with friends in the car. You might also consider restricting the time of day when teens may drive (at first).

Outlaw drag racing, off-road stunts, eating while driving, ear-splitting volume on the radio, and insist that your kids wear seat belts at all times.

Some parents offer their kids "good guy" auto insurance. They get a reduction in their insurance premium if they can maintain a B average in school, a good driving record, etc. If your teen gets a ticket or their grades slip, you can say, "Gee, that's a shame. Now your insurance rates are going to go up. How do you plan to cover the increase?"

Most auto policies have a deductible amount, usually $250 or $500.

Require your teenager to make a "deposit" in your bank account equal to the amount of the deductible before he or she can drive. If there's an accident, it will be used to repair the car. Of course, in order for the teenager to drive again, another deposit will have to be made.

Don't forget to talk about drinking and driving. Establish a zero-tolerance policy on this. If anyone drives their car under the influence, driving privileges will be suspended indefinitely, and their car will no longer be available to them, period. Hopefully your kids will never test you on this, but if you don't make your position very clear, they might.

As with most things, the best way to insure that your kids will be good drivers is to set a good example for them when you drive. Wear your seat belts, obey traffic laws, never drive under the influence, and never engage in "road rage." Parents have an obligation to model good driving behavior for their teenagers.

Raise a Hope Addict, Not a Dope Addict

There's more than just saying no.

I'm not going to provide you with the latest statistics on teen drug abuse, a comprehensive list of drugs your kids may be using, ten ways to tell if your kids have been using them, or even what to do if you discover they are. To be honest, I'm not an expert on any of that.

None of my children used drugs while they were teenagers, but I have spent countless hours praying and counseling with parents who were not so blessed. I'm well aware of the fact that drug abuse is a terrible scourge that can destroy families and ruin the lives of bright, beautiful kids. Whatever you can do to reduce the likelihood of your kids abusing drugs, you should do it. It is a very serious matter indeed.

Growing Up in a Drug Culture

We all know that more kids are using drugs today than ever before, and I include alcohol on my list of drugs. Not all who use them are addicted, but many are. We hear a lot about teenagers and drugs—as if drugs were as much a part of youth culture as MTV, yellow hair, and navel rings—but that's not really true. The fact is that drugs are a big part of American culture in general.

Teenagers use drugs because adults do. A close look at the statistics will show that despite what you hear, the percentage of teens who use drugs is no greater than the percentage of adults who do. Teens can't be singled out as the nation's drug abusers. There is a teen drug problem in America because there is an adult drug problem in America.

We also hear a lot about kids and drugs today because they are much more available than ever before. Despite the government's "war on drugs" and the many programs designed to create "drug-free zones" for our kids, drugs are easier to find than ever before, and teenagers do find them. When I graduated from high school in 1963, I didn't know a single classmate of mine who used drugs. Anyone who graduated after 1963 has a different story to tell. The drug epidemic among young people in this country emerged very quickly, and it continues today.

What You Can Do

You can reduce the likelihood that your kids will use or abuse drugs, but you can't do anything at all to guarantee they won't. There's no way to prevent teenagers from making bad choices. All that has been said so far in this book about trusting your kids and giving them space enough to learn and grow (even from their mistakes) applies to drugs and alcohol as well. Ultimately, your kids have to decide for themselves how they will respond to the drug culture that is part of their world.

But here are some things you *can* do:

1. *Set a good example.* I know I'm preaching to the choir here, since parents who set bad examples generally don't buy parenting books, but remember that if you abuse drugs or alcohol, there's a strong likelihood your kids will too.
2. *Don't overmedicate your kids.* Do you head for the medicine chest whenever your kids (or you) have an ache or pain? Be careful. You may inadvertently be teaching your kids that pain is always to be avoided (which it's not) and that the way to alleviate pain is to self-medicate. Kids should learn that life is not always pain-free and that pain often is God's way of telling us that we need to make some changes in our lives. Again, this is something we can teach by example.

3. *Talk about drugs with your kids, but communicate trust.* I sometimes worry about all those ads that keep encouraging parents to talk frequently with kids about drugs. Certainly you shouldn't be silent on the subject, but you don't want to communicate to your kids that you don't trust them or that they are stupid. If you make it clear in word and deed that the use of drugs and alcohol are not acceptable in your family, they'll get the message.

4. *Avoid demonizing drugs.* There's no need to get so hysterical about drugs that we blow them out of proportion. Don't get me wrong—drug and alcohol abuse is extremely dangerous and needs to be dealt with forcefully. But when kids hear us preaching a harsher, scarier antisubstance line than the true dangers warrant, we risk a credibility gap. Most kids know that it's possible to smoke a joint and not get addicted. They may even be aware that their parents did so without any harmful effects—at least none that they can see. They may have friends who use drugs, and they seem fine. While none of this justifies the use of drugs, kids sometimes get the impression that we are lying to them, so they don't listen at all. There are plenty of good reasons for kids to stay away from drugs and alcohol, so there's no need to use scare tactics. They can understand their responsibility to obey the laws of the land. They can understand why drinking and driving don't mix. They can understand that mind- or mood-altering drugs are addictive and can interfere with their ability to make good decisions and achieve success in life. By being clear with kids about the real dangers of drugs and alcohol, your kids will be in a better position to make wise, informed decisions.

5. *Encourage healthy friendship choices.* As we discussed earlier, pay close attention to whom your kids hang out with. Influence their influencers. Peer pressure doesn't cause addiction, but it can lead to experimentation. If your teenager's primary social group uses drugs for partying or other recreational use, it's likely that your teen will also try drugs or use them occasionally. You can't choose your kids' friends for them, but if you can get them involved in a church that has an active youth ministry, there's a good chance they'll find friends who don't need drugs to have a good time. Researchers have confirmed that kids who are involved in church youth groups are far less likely to become drug abusers.

More Than Just Saying No

If our heavenly Father couldn't prevent Adam and Eve from eating forbidden fruit in the Garden of Eden, neither can you prevent your kids from ingesting things they shouldn't, and that includes drugs and alcohol. They will need a whole lot more than lectures, rules, or slogans to resist the lure of harmful substances. What they need is self-respect, self-confidence, self-reliance, and a positive, hopeful outlook on life.

Many parents today look for a magic formula that will keep their kids off drugs, but there really is none. If teens don't have the inner strength to say no to harmful things on their own, there's not much you can do to keep them from saying yes.

Hope That Lasts

Drug-resistant kids are those who are high on hope. And there is no greater hope than the hope that comes from knowing Jesus Christ. I love to talk to teenagers about Christian hope because it differs so completely from that based on wishful thinking, personal success, technology, the economy, the government, or other human accomplishments. Christian hope doesn't depend on what might happen, but our hope is based on what has already happened. It rests entirely on the finished work of Jesus Christ. Our hope is secure in the knowledge that Christ has absolutely guaranteed our future.

It is that kind of hope that has the power to sustain our kids and to give them victory over temptation. Again, that's why it's so important to give our kids the benefit of a home built on the strong foundation of faith in Christ. I'm not saying that Christian kids are immune to drug abuse, but there's no question that kids who know Jesus are much less likely to choose drugs over the hope they have in Christ. Unlike drugs, Christian hope doesn't disappoint us (Romans 5:5). It's the only hope worth getting hooked on.

Learn the Art of Stealth Communication

Bad breath is better than no breath at all.

Hey, Chris, what's up?"

"Not much, Dad. Just thinking."

"Anything I can help you with?"

"Well, I don't know. I'm just worried about school and grades and stuff. No matter how hard I try, I just can't seem to get the hang of algebra and political science. And if I don't get As in those two classes, I can kiss that scholarship good-bye."

"You know, Son, I had a hard time in high school myself. There were so many distractions . . . sports and girls and all my extracurricular activities. But once I put my mind to it, I decided to really concentrate on the subjects giving me trouble and things turned out okay. I didn't get As like you probably will, but I did better than I thought I would."

"Thanks, Dad. It's great to hear how things were when you were my age. Maybe I can start concentrating a little more and pull my grades up just like you did."

◆ ◆ ◆

The above conversation is—as you might have guessed—a work of fiction. It never took place and probably never will.

Most actual conversations between parents and teenagers go more like this:

"Chris, turn off the TV and get busy on your homework."

"Unnghh."

Or:

"Dad, can I have ten bucks?"

"Unnghh."

Let's face it. It's not easy to talk to teenagers. That's why most conversations don't last very long. Sometimes talking with teenagers can be like walking through a minefield. Say the wrong thing and *kaboom*. But just because communication between parents and teenagers lacks both quantity and quality isn't necessarily a sign that anything is wrong. It's normal for conversations to be one-sided, with the parents doing most of the talking.

There's an old saying about bad breath being better than no breath at all. It's true. We can't stop talking to kids just because our communication with them is less than warm and fuzzy all the time. Sometimes we get so frustrated by our communication flops that we just stop trying. But it's better to communicate and fail than not to communicate at all. And actually, we may think we have failed when we haven't at all. You may exit a conversation feeling frustrated or upset, but your teenager may not feel any of that. He or she has moved on to other things.

So if you are waiting for that day when all conversations with your kids are pleasant and uplifting, don't hold your breath. They never will be, but so what? Most kids eventually grow up appreciating the fact that their parents took the time to nag them about their behavior when they deserved it. At least the parents cared enough to do it, as unpleasant as it may have been at the time.

Talking to a Brick Wall

"Tanya, if I were you, I'd apply for a job at Art Mart. They're hiring for the summer, and since you like art so much, I think that would be a good place for you to work."

"Mom, leave me alone. We've had this conversation before."

"No, Tanya, you really need to get a job."

"Mom, I don't want to work at Art Mart! Besides, I told you that Jennifer's dad has a friend who is going to get us jobs at Six Flags. I don't need to go looking for a job."

"But you don't have one yet."

"I will. Just leave me alone."

One week later:

"Mom, guess what! I'm getting a job at Art Mart! I was talking to my design teacher this morning, and she said that Art Mart was hiring her students. She knows the manager and gave me his number. I called, and he said to just come by and fill out an application!"

"What did I say to you just last week?"

"I don't remember."

This is one aspect of parent-teen communication that can be particularly frustrating. As adults, we believe that we are wiser than our kids, that we have gone through it all before, and that we can offer them some important advice that will enrich their lives.

But teenagers are unlikely to hear us, even when we are right and when our words are obviously in their own best interest. They might listen to someone else, as in Tanya's case, or they will just ignore us and do the opposite of what we tell them in order to feel like they are making their own decisions. If things don't work out and they suffer the consequences—proving the parent right—they still have a hard time acknowledging the wisdom of their parents. This was to them an exception, proving nothing.

Teenagers believe that to take the advice of their parents compromises their independence. To take parental advice and to recognize its helpfulness feels like defeat. It's a defeat of all they are trying to do—to prove they can make decisions on their own. For a teenager to make a right decision based on parental advice is often less desirable than making a bad decision on their own.

That doesn't mean that you shouldn't keep trying. You don't want to argue with them or waste your breath trying to convince them to see things your way—but you still need to give advice, set limits, and enforce consequences. If you see them getting into trouble, you should warn them about it. You do have a powerful influence on your kids, even when there seems to be evidence to the contrary. When your kids get older and their adulthood becomes more established, they will begin to appreciate your point of view and listen more intentionally.

Stealth Communication

"It was weird. Dad and I drove over to Aunt Betty's to help her move. On the way home in the car, we just started talking. About all kinds of stuff. I don't think I've ever talked with Dad like that in my whole life. I mean, I actually saw him as a regular person. It was kind of neat, but it was also kind of weird."

◆ ◆ ◆

To communicate successfully with a teenager is to be patient. Sometimes you will have surprisingly positive conversations with your kids, but they are hard to predict and they can't be forced. They happen when they happen. Planning to have a conversation is fine, but you also have to accept that it may not turn out the way you planned.

For six years, I took my son Nathan out to breakfast once a week so that we could have marvelous conversations over our bacon and eggs. But I quickly learned that it takes two to tango. More often than not, we had short snippets of talk—not quite conversation, not very deep or interesting—but usually civil. Sometimes we just didn't have much to say at all.

But just because good conversation doesn't take place every time doesn't mean you stop trying. I learned to be grateful for those few-and-far-between chances my kids gave me to share my heart with them or to listen intently to what was on theirs.

Stealth communication is trusting that even though communication with your teenager is often difficult, it does in fact happen. You can increase the odds of it happening by spending more time with your kids, talking in pleasant rather than preachy tones, accentuating the positive, avoiding cutting remarks, and using humor. Your efforts will pay eventual dividends.

Your Voice, Their Language

The art of stealth communication is also the art of learning to communicate in the language your teenager understands best. That doesn't mean you have to use the latest teen slang or become a stand-up comic. In fact you may not have to speak at all.

Some parents communicate best with their kids by writing letters or notes to them. Most kids hear better with their eyes than with their ears. Some parents like to sneak notes into their teen's school lunch, hide them in their sock drawer, or plant one under their pillow. You can mail them or deliver them in person. If you prefer, use e-mail, although I prefer good old paper and ink. If writing is difficult for you, try putting messages on audio- or videotapes.

Perhaps you enjoy writing poems or songs. I know several parents who communicate best with their kids by composing poetry. You can communicate with drawings, photographs, cartoons, jokes, and stories. And they don't have to be original with you. If you hear a song on the radio that expresses how you feel, a story that touches your heart, or a joke that makes you laugh, just share it with your kids. It's not surprising that kids often treasure these kinds of communications and keep them for years.

Every young person has his or her own unique way of responding to what they hear, see, and experience. Some are visual learners, others are auditory. Some are feelers; others are thinkers. As parents, we need to understand and appreciate the language our kids speak best and then find a voice to match it. Too often, we tend to communicate primarily in our own language— what is most comfortable for us—rather than theirs. Use a variety of communication styles with your kids. Trial and error, experimentation, and persistence will lead you to some truly inspired moments when you will connect and come through loud and clear.

38

Be Ready to Listen When They're Ready to Talk

If you ever feel somewhat out of touch with your teenager, learn to listen.

I'll expect you home at midnight."

"Oh, Mom, come on. Nobody gets home that early, nobody! Do you want me to be the only kid there who has to leave early? The only one who can't stay out? Do you? Do you want me to ruin everybody else's time because I have to leave because my mom doesn't trust me while everybody else's mom does? Is that what you want? Is it?"

"Just be home by midnight."

"Come on, Mom, just this once. Please, pretty please. I never have any fun; I really don't. You never let me do anything. Never! If you had your way, I'd be in jail. You know you're ruining my life. Probably no one will ever invite me anywhere again as long as I live. I'll spend the rest of my life in my room. Is that what you want? I hope you're happy; I really hope so. Maybe I won't even go. I mean, what's the point? I have to come home before the concert's even started."

"As long as you're home at midnight you can do what you want."

"Mom, you're not listening to me!"

Listening When Setting Limits

Kids like to complain that their parents don't listen to them. Usually that's when parents are setting or enforcing limits and teenagers are arguing and complaining about them. But no parent wants to listen to a whining, belligerent teenager. It's exhausting, emotionally draining, and most often counterproductive. Whenever kids badger their parents into arguments, the real challenge is not to listen but to stay calm, firm, and focused. Listening isn't required so much as perseverance is.

There are times, however, when teenagers really do have something important to say. They believe they have relevant information that may influence you to change your mind. They just want a chance to be heard—to plead their case.

◆ ◆ ◆

"Mom, I know that it means staying out past my curfew, but the featured band won't even start playing until eleven, and that's the band I really want to hear. I'll be with Melissa, Jennifer, and Danielle, and Jennifer's dad has agreed to pick us all up at twelve-thirty when it's over. It's totally safe. I know it's late, but I don't have school the next day."

◆ ◆ ◆

There's no reason why you shouldn't at least listen to your teenager if he or she is genuinely trying to reason with you rather than wear you down. You can usually tell when kids want to communicate rather than argue. Raucous, abusive, accusatory, or insulting language is not an invitation to a discussion, but to a dogfight.

If your teenager is willing to speak respectfully, then you should be willing to listen respectfully. If his or her argument is reasonable, give it genuine consideration and make a decision. You can change your mind without having your authority eroded, and you'll score some points for your relationship. But you don't want to just cave in. Listening doesn't mean letting kids have their way. If the argument doesn't hold water, or if you have valid reasons for sticking with your original decision, then let your teenager know the verdict and move on. Listen, retain your authority, and avoid arguing.

Listening to teenagers while setting their limits is appropriate, but this is not true for establishing boundaries for younger children. To listen to children while setting limits is to invite disaster. It does no good to enter into a discussion with a small child about the relative merits of a decision that you have made. What the child hears is an invitation to keep on fussing until you get so frustrated you'll finally give in to their demands. They will throw tantrums and say anything to get their way, and if you pay any real attention to them, you only prolong the agony. Consulting with children regarding rules and limits is a sure way to raise demanding, self-centered, out-of-control kids. Unilateral authority must be exercised.

But with adolescents, the situation changes. As their adulthood emerges, so does their need to be taken seriously. It's often hard for parents to make that shift from unilateral to mutual authority with teenagers, but not being willing to listen invites disaster. Teenagers can't and won't be ignored.

Why should a parent give respect to her teenager when the teen doesn't give it in return? Doesn't matter. The parent is the adult while the teenager is the adult-in-training. Respect is learned when it is given. While it doesn't happen overnight, kids do learn how to be respectful by being treated respectfully.

Listening When They Want to Talk

There are other times, however, when kids just want to talk. They aren't trying to change your mind or get anything from you. They want to tell you about something that happened to them, their experiences, their concerns, their problems, their fears. Sometimes they want to tell you about things you do that really bother them. Sometimes they want advice. Sometimes they want encouragement. In any event, teenagers do have a need to communicate with their parents from time to time.

If your kids don't communicate much with you, it's possible that they have simply given up trying. One of the reasons why today's kids are content to speak in the shrugs, grunts, and code language of youth culture is because they see no point in trying to talk like an adult. Why should they? There are no adults in their lives who will listen to them.

When we listen to our teenagers, we assure them that they are valued, that what they have to say is important. One of the reasons so many kids today have a hard time *praying* is because no one listens to them. It's hard for teenagers to believe that the Creator of the universe will listen to them when their own parents won't. When we listen to our kids, we are demonstrating the love of God. We are modeling it for them. It has been said that "listening is the language of love." Maybe that's why God gave us two ears and one mouth. Listening often communicates more than talking does. When we stop what we are doing and really pay attention to what another person has to say, we are saying more with our ears than we ever could with our mouths.

If you ever feel somewhat out of touch with your kids, learn to listen. Let your teenager know, "If there ever is something that you want to talk about, I will listen." Many adolescents may never take their parents up on an offer like that, but letting your kids know that you are available to listen can be very encouraging to a teenager.

If necessary, schedule some time to be with your teenager so that you can give him or her your undivided attention. Have breakfast or lunch together, make the dinner table a good time of sharing, date your kids, or find other times to be with them just to talk and listen to each other. The more you do it, the easier it will get. And remember that listening means *listening,* not giving advice or sitting in judgment. If you tell your kids that you will listen, then by all means listen.

Listening is a skill that everybody can get better at. There are dozens of books on the market which teach parents such methods as active listening, reflective listening, and attentive listening, but one of the simplest and most helpful strategies I've learned is called FAD. It's an acronym that stands for *focus, accept, and draw out.*

Focus means stop whatever you're doing and give the person your complete attention. Put the paper down, turn off the TV or radio, face the person, make eye contact, and zero in.

Accept means to empathize with the person who is speaking, to feel his emotion. Sometimes we communicate this with body language, leaning forward, expressing appropriate emotions, responding to what they have to say.

Draw out means ask questions, probe, and explore what the person is saying to you. Communicate to the person speaking that you are so interested that you want more information. Like the performer who gets an encore, a speaker who is encouraged to share more feels affirmed and loved.

FAD is a great way to listen, and it communicates the kind of respect and positive high regard that teenagers need.

39

Give Them a Shot at Changing the World

I've never been the answer to anybody's prayers before.

When the little wooden church was burned to the ground by vandals, the young Mexican pastor and his poor congregation knew it might take years—if ever—before they could rebuild. They had neither money nor building materials. All they could do was pray for a miracle.

They got their miracle in the form of a youth group from San Diego who heard about the church fire in Ensenada and responded by sending a work crew. In five days during spring break of 1997, six high-school students and two adult leaders completely rebuilt that little church on its old foundation. While other students were off partying in places like Palm Springs and Rosarito Beach, these kids were being the answer to somebody's prayers.

Many people find it hard to believe that today's kids would do that. But every year tens of thousands of teenagers give up their Easter or summer vacations to serve God all over the world. Even more incredibly, they often do it while enduring long bus trips, extreme weather, bad food, sleeping in tents, no bathrooms, no running water, no electricity, no privacy, no entertainment, no pay—in exchange for some backbreaking work.

Over the years, my wife and I have accompanied dozens of youth groups on mission trips and work projects of every description. I'm always impressed with how eager teenagers can be to give of themselves. Sometimes it's a challenge to get kids to go on that first trip, but once they have tasted the deep satisfaction that comes from making a positive difference in someone else's life, they invariably get hooked on it. I know many adults in Christian service today who had their first real ministry experience on a youth group mission trip.

Kids don't have to be involved with a church youth group to get involved in service, however. Our family has participated in programs sponsored by all kinds of social-service agencies, mission organizations, and community programs—and some things we have just done on our own. For example, we had a family project called "Project Cinderella" which involved buying shoes for children living in the poorest neighborhoods around Tijuana, Mexico. Every year, we loaded up our minivan with new shoes of all sizes and took them across the border to match them up with the feet of children, many of whom were getting their first new pair of shoes. Not only did we touch the lives of those Mexican children in a significant way, but our own kids' lives were deeply impacted. It's not surprising that our daughter chose to work with abused and neglected children as a career when she graduated from college.

Fringe Benefits

The intended purpose of mission, service, and volunteer work is of course to contribute to the lives of others or to the world. But more often than not, the benefits gained by those doing the work far exceed the actual work that has been done.

For example, kids who serve learn more about compassion than they could ever learn in a classroom. When kids have their hearts broken by the things that break the heart of God, they learn what it means to care deeply for those who are in need.

They also learn about gratitude. I have seen countless youth come home from mission trips with their attitudes completely changed regarding material possessions. They begin to appreciate what they have and how blessed they really are. And they almost always learn that being rich and being happy have nothing at all to do with each other.

They learn about humility and relationships. Teenagers never look more beautiful than they do after a few days without their makeup kits, jewelry, hair dryers, showers, designer clothes, and all the accouterment of adolescence that give them status. When the masks come off and kids start being authentic, they open up to each other and community is formed.

They learn about responsibility and commitment. When kids are given an important task and complete it without being nagged by their parents, they gain confidence in themselves and discover talents and abilities they never knew they had.

They also gain a sense of significance. Most teens today feel like they are burdens to society rather than contributors to it. By serving others, they learn that there is a place for them in the world and that God can really use them to make a difference.

If your kids get involved in ministry and service, their lives will be changed. And those changes—which are always for the better—will inevitably be carried with them into adulthood. Without exception, my greatest heroes are adults who learned to give of themselves when they were teenagers.

What in the World Can a Kid Do?

There are many ways for kids to serve, but you can't really force them to do anything they don't want to do.

The best way to encourage kids to serve is to get involved in service yourself, especially while your children are young. You might consider supporting a needy child through a child sponsorship program like Compassion International or World Vision. Perhaps you could volunteer as a family to help serve meals on Thanksgiving at a local homeless shelter. You could go Christmas caroling at hospitals, convalescent homes, or the homes of shutins. These are just a few of the things our family has done that have helped our kids develop a heart for serving others.

Encourage your church's youth ministry to do more mission and service activities rather than spending thousands of dollars on summer camps and recreational activities designed primarily to entertain. If the youth leaders aren't capable of planning them, there are numerous organizations that work with local church youth groups to help plan mission trips both at home and in many foreign countries.

Encourage your teenager to consider going alone or with a friend on a short-term mission trip abroad. Our daughter served one summer in Belize doing missionary work. Perhaps there are places close to home where your kids could combine a summer job with ministry. All three of our kids worked at Christian summer camps doing everything from being cabin counselors to cleaning toilets. Since they were getting little or no pay for their work, we helped subsidize them so that they could have that experience.

There is hardly anything that teenagers can't do to impact their world. Conducting food or clothing drives for the homeless, installing smoke alarms in the homes of the poor, doing yard- or housework for shut-ins, baby-sitting for parents who can't afford it, and putting up Christmas lights on the homes of senior citizens—literally, the sky's the limit. Don't let your kids grow up without having the opportunity to serve somebody.

Help Them Find
a Job with Benefits

If I ever work at Burger Boy again, just shoot me.

Just as pilots-in-training need flight simulators, so teenagers need experience in the real world to practice being responsible and accountable to someone other than their parents.

That's why it's good for teenagers to work outside the home, to have jobs.

This is a scary issue for some parents. They worry that maybe their teen is too young, that a job will interfere with their schoolwork, or that the money they earn will be spent on harmful things. Are jobs bad for teens?

Until recent times, almost all teenagers had jobs whether they wanted one or not. In the past, all young people who were big enough and strong enough to work had jobs either on the farm or in the factory, working right alongside adults. In some countries this is still true.

There is nothing wrong with giving young people a chance to be useful, to contribute to their families, or to learn a new skill. In the most civilized of nations down through history, it was common for youngsters to leave home—often when they were quite young—to live and work for "masters" who would teach them a trade in exchange for their labor. If they stuck to it and did a good job, they would learn trade secrets that would grant them supervised entry into the adult world and enable them to become successful in business themselves. The world has changed, of course, and apprenticeships have been replaced by compulsory education. Still, it's important to note that teenagers were quite capable then—as they are now—of doing meaningful work.

Child-labor laws and the invention of adolescence pretty much ended youth employment in the first half of the twentieth century in America. But in the last fifty years, there has been a steady increase in the number of adolescents who work at jobs while they attend school. In the 1940s, only about 4 percent of teenagers had jobs. Today, more than 75 percent do. The proliferation of retail stores and fast-food restaurants has opened up millions of part-time jobs at minimum wages that have been snatched up by kids who now make up a huge market for consumer goods. Trendy clothing, electronics, music, movies, and other leisure activities are no match for the traditional weekly allowance, so more and more kids are lured into the job market to make money to acquire the ever-increasing amenities of teen culture.

If I Ever Work at Burger Boy Again, Just Shoot Me

Teen work is good, but the vast majority of jobs available to teens today bear little resemblance to apprenticeships of the past. Instead, they tend to be menial, repetitive jobs that depend not at all on a youth's interests, talents, abilities, or career goals. Further, teens who work long hours often have difficulty managing their time and balancing their family life, school life, social life, and extracurricular activities. Research has confirmed that teens who work more than twenty hours per week generally miss more school, spend less time on homework, and get lower grades. This can be a real concern for parents.

A part-time job during the school year or a full-time summer job can be a rewarding and educational experience for a teenager. A job can teach a kid how to secure and hold a job, how to budget and manage time and money, how to communicate well with bosses, fellow employees, and the public.

The greatest benefit of teen jobs, however, is the opportunity for kids to assume some real responsibility. When they are required to show up on time, follow instructions, perform tasks, and handle other people's money, they become more responsible people. When kids have to be responsible in a job situation, they are more likely to become responsible elsewhere—like at home or school.

If nothing else, teen jobs teach kids firsthand about the buying power of low-income wages. They'll discover how little they can actually purchase with a burger-flipper paycheck. That can be a real bonus to parents who may have tried unsuccessfully to motivate their teenagers to get good grades and prepare themselves for a promising career. Most kids who work at fast-food restaurants as teenagers vow to never return.

Finding a Job with Benefits

If your teenager can show that he or she is capable of juggling the demands of holding down a job with other obligations, such as family time (mealtimes), church time, school time, and homework, then there's no reason why your teen shouldn't have a job. Most states require students to be sixteen years old to seek employment.

But encourage him or her to find one with *benefits*. By benefits, I don't mean health insurance, overtime pay, or 401K plans. I'm referring instead to opportunities to further one's career plans, to learn a new skill or trade, to make a contribution to the world, to develop character and self-discipline and similar benefits. There are better jobs out there than most kids realize. You just have to go out and find them.

When I was in high school looking toward architecture as a career, I not only worked for my dad, a building contractor, but I got a part-time job as a blueprint boy in an architectural firm. I was basically a lackey for all the draftsmen who needed someone to run errands for them, but it was a great learning experience to peer over their shoulders and watch them work.

Encourage your kids to be entrepreneurial. There are many kids who start their own small businesses mowing lawns, doing housework, plowing snow, repairing computers, or tutoring children. Our daughter learned to cut hair, so her Christmas gift from us one year was a pair of electric clippers and other hair-cutting tools. She practically put herself through college cutting the hair of her friends. Our son Corey tried his hand as an independent seller of premium kitchen knives one summer. We were skeptical at first, but the job allowed Corey to set his own schedule and develop communication skills we never knew he possessed. He sold knives to just about everybody we knew (including us) and made a significant sum of money.

Before your teenager starts looking for a job, agree ahead of time on the rules and set some limits. How many hours a week can he/she work? (I recommend no more than fifteen during the school year for full-time students.) Will he/she work during the day, evenings, or weekends? What about Sunday mornings? (At our house, the answer was no.) What kinds of jobs are acceptable or unacceptable? What about schoolwork? (If grades drop, the job gets dropped.) What is the purpose of the job? How will the income be used? You will need to clarify all these issues with your teenager before the job search begins.

Should kids help cover their own living expenses? Absolutely. Teens shouldn't use their income simply to pay for entertainment, snacks, gizmos, and gadgets. If they are driving, they should assume more of their auto expenses, including insurance. If they want to wear designer clothes, they can pay for those items. This is a good way for kids to learn independence and self-reliance. Don't be afraid to let your kids work.

Provide Them with Landing Gear

There's no way my child will survive without someone to pick up after him, make sure he eats right, and do his laundry.

As your kids head off into the wild blue yonder of adulthood, you'll probably have worries about the prospects of your kids living in a world without curfews, vegetables, or clean laundry. After all, for eighteen years or more, you have provided everything they needed, and now they will have to take care of themselves. You won't be there to make sure they have what they need, that they're doing things the right way, or that they're getting all the right information. They won't have you and your lifetime of experience to help them. They'll be on their own. That's scary.

But if you have been raising your kids to be responsible and have resisted micromanaging their lives, they'll probably be fine once they take flight. They'll figure things out, make a few mistakes, and learn things the hard way, just like you did. Like many kids who make up today's point-and-click generation, yours will undoubtedly experience some frustration and disappointments when things don't automatically work out the way they had expected, but they'll survive.

Still, you can help your kids avoid crash-landings by equipping them with some of the facts of life that every adult needs to survive on his or her own in the real world. There are all kinds of mundane life details that parents often fail to bring up with their teens. After they are gone, you suddenly realize that you never got a chance to sit down and tell them what they need to know. Or they call frantically from some faraway place, wondering why they are getting registered mail from the Internal Revenue Service. What's this all about?

What do your kids need to learn before they leave home? Certainly an exhaustive list of things to cover would take a book all by itself. In fact, there are several books that I can recommend, including *So You Want to Move Out? A Guide to Living on Your Own* by Rik Feeney and *The Teenager's Guide to the Real World* by Marshall Brain. Both of these books were written for teenagers, and they cover everything from how to dress for a job interview to preparing a will.

It's possible that your teenager has learned some basic survival skills in school if they have taken courses like home economics. Even so, they don't cover everything, and kids still need to hear from their parents. Listed below are a few "landing gear" items you can discuss with your young adult, about-to-leave-home teenager. While not exhaustive, this list gives you an idea of the kinds of issues that need to be covered.

How to find, secure, and hold a job. If your teenager has held a job already, then he or she may have learned most of what they need to know about this subject by experience. But make sure they are familiar with the process of applying for jobs, filling out application forms, preparing for interviews, writing résumés, asking the right questions about working conditions and benefits, understanding paycheck stubs, deductions, retirement plans, and unions.

How to find affordable housing. At some point your offspring will need to find a place to live. Discuss with them their housing options. What will they be able to afford? An apartment? Condo? A house for rent? A room for rent? Furnished or unfurnished? What about utilities? What's involved in buying a house or a condo? You can give your kids an advantage by helping them understand rental and lease agreements, contracts, security deposits, renter's insurance, and other housing issues.

How to establish credit. Most young people don't realize that the best time to get a loan is when you don't need one. If you can apply for a small loan and pay it back on time, you will establish a credit history that will make it possible to get credit when you need it. Credit problems often loom large for young people who are just starting out. Kids should know the importance of paying bills on time, avoiding late fees and high interest rates, and how to manage credit or debit cards.

How to file an income tax return. Filing that first tax return can be an intimidating experience for young people who don't know what they are doing. Help them understand the IRS, the 1040, the W-2, the 1099, and all those other mysterious numbers and letters. Teach them the importance of keeping good records and being honest.

How to stay healthy. Okay, your kids probably won't listen very well about nutrition, exercising, getting enough sleep, and getting regular medical and dental checkups, but make sure they appreciate the fact that all the money and success in the world means nothing at all if you aren't healthy. There are millionaires who would gladly trade every dime they ever made for a few days of good health.

How to save money. Some kids are shocked when they discover that money doesn't just come spewing out of an ATM machine anytime you want it. You can teach your kids how to save money by shopping for bargains, using coupons, finding free stuff, saving energy, avoiding scams, saving on telephone bills, Internet service, and other utilities. Your teen also needs to learn about the difference between savings accounts, CDs (not the music kind), money-market funds, mutual funds, IRA accounts, and other ways to save or invest.

Check Out Their
Flight Plan

We can help our kids be among those who really find joy in serving God in their chosen occupations.

D ad, I think I've decided to become a professional banjo player." Don't laugh. I almost did that. But thankfully, I realized that making a living playing a banjo is like making a living playing sports. You had better be really, really good. I still play a banjo—but for fun, not for money. There's a joke that goes, "How do you get a banjo player off your front porch?" Answer: "Pay for the pizza."

Do you ever wonder what your son or daughter is going to do for a living?

As your kids approach the end of high school and look toward college, they really should have some idea of what their life's work will be, even though it may change. Some young people have a pretty clear idea of what career they would like to pursue, but most do not. Our rapidly changing world has contributed to much of the confusion and procrastination on the part of today's kids, but lack of guidance and direction from parents is also a major factor.

When kids enter college without a career plan, the likelihood of their dropping out of college increases significantly. Most freshmen learn this fact during their college orientation when the dean asks them to look at the person to their right, then their left, then to look at themselves. "One of you will not be here by the end of the year," he solemnly declares.

Other students manage to graduate, but with degrees that are only marginally useful. Given the enormous costs of a college education these days, it's simply not very smart to attend college without any career goals in mind. I know one frustrated couple whose daughter recently moved back home after getting her degree in psychology from a top university. Four years and over a hundred thousand dollars of her parents' money later, she's not sure she wants to go into psychology after all. She's thinking now about becoming a hair stylist.

It's not unusual for students to change their minds or their majors (I changed mine four times), but if they don't have anything in mind at all, chances are they will drift and find college to be a frustrating and unrewarding experience. With career goals, however, students have something to shoot for. They can choose the right major and the electives that will help them to achieve those goals.

Your kids are uniquely gifted to do some things really well and other things not so well. Choosing a career that matches up well with their dreams and abilities can be a real challenge. According to *The Dictionary of Occupational Titles* published by the U.S. Department of Labor, there are more than twenty thousand occupations to choose from. Compare that with the not-too-distant past when kids usually worked in the same job as their parents and young women had few, if any, choices.

Our role as parents is not to help our kids find the perfect career, but we should help them discover one that they can get excited about and pursue with confidence. Many parents either push their kids toward a career they don't really want, or they just avoid the subject altogether. It's not enough to just tell kids they can be anything they want to be. We need to explore with them what they really want to do, then point them toward the best route to those goals.

Thinking through a Career

Here are some ways you can help your kids choose the right career.

Teach them the difference between their vocation and their occupation—in other words, their *calling* and their *job*. There are hundreds of thousands of jobs out there, but only one calling for each individual. Your calling is what you were meant to do. Ask yourself, what do I really enjoy doing? What gets me excited? What brings me happiness and fulfillment? Questions like these can give you some clues if not the final answer. From the Christian perspective, your vocation is what God created you to do.

Teach them not to choose a life's work based on how much it pays. In today's world, money is the basis of too many important decisions. A lawyer friend of mine told me recently that his son was graduating next year from law school and that he had already been offered a position at the top law firm in Los Angeles with a starting salary of $360,000 per year. After catching my breath, I proudly told him that my son is thriving as a youth pastor at a church in Orange County. I wanted to tell him that my son is making less than one-tenth of what his son will make, but I decided not to embarrass him with that information. I'm very proud that my kids are doing what they feel called to do, not what pays the most.

Young people need to learn from their parents that if you don't enjoy what you're doing, there's not enough money in the world to compensate for that. But if you love what you do, then you are already rich. If you love what you do, money will come. You can trust God for that.

Ask your kids, "Who do you admire most? Who would you like to be like?" Sometimes God puts particular people in our paths to inspire us to do what He wants us to do. I chose to go into youth ministry because of several men who made a big impression on me when I was a young man. I was so impressed with their creativity, their ability to communicate with kids, their love for God, and their love for what they were doing that I wanted to be just like them.

Encourage them to do a little career shopping. Talk to people in a variety of professions to find out what their jobs are like and how they settled for that career. Most people love to talk about their jobs and to tell their stories. Most adults are usually happy to help a youth get started on the right path. There's no substitute for talking to people and learning firsthand what it takes to work in a specific profession.

Encourage your kids to pray about their future work. In fact, pray with them. Ask God to give them direction and guidance, so that they can do His will, not yours or anybody else's.

Help them to understand that for the Christian, work and worship are the same thing. That is, the purpose of work is to glorify God, just as worship is. That's why the Bible uses those two words interchangeably. As Paul put it, "Whatever you do, work at it with all your heart, as working for the Lord, not for men" (Colossians 3:23).

Studies show that more than 70 percent of all workers in the United States find their jobs either boring, stressful, or unsatisfying. Most can't wait to retire so they can do what they really want to do. With some guidance and prayer support, we can help our kids be among those who really find joy in serving God in their chosen occupation.

Help Them Get
a Higher Education

A certain level of performance should be required in exchange for a tuition check.

For many seventeen- and eighteen-year-olds going to college is the first big step toward achieving true independence. It's also a big step for parents. Many kids go away to college and never return home, at least not for any length of time. When our youngest left for college, my wife and I looked at each other and realized that we were alone. We were finished. Our nest was empty.

But college students don't leave completely. They keep a toehold at home, at least for a while. They return to their old bedrooms during breaks or for the summer. They still rely on parents for financial support and other necessities. If your kids are college material, you should make it possible for them to go. Ideally, it's best if they can go away to college so that they can experience dorm life rather than living at home with Mom and Dad.

College isn't for everyone, however. While it can be a positive experience as well as necessary preparation for a career, a college degree is no longer a guarantee of getting a good job. In fact, it's about equal to what a high-school diploma represented a generation or two ago. If your son or daughter doesn't have clarity or at least some leanings toward their interests and career goals, it may be best for them to wait until they do.

But once your son or daughter has a direction in mind, you can narrow down the field of colleges, universities, or technical training schools that will best help them reach their goals.

When our daughter was still a junior in high school, we did a college tour as a family vacation. We visited half a dozen colleges in several different states so that she could make an informed decision about where to go. Colleges are like any other business or product; it's a good idea to comparison-shop to find the best school. Once we knew which schools best suited her needs, our daughter began the application process.

Worth the Trouble

There are many good reasons to go to college, the most obvious is to further one's career goals. Some careers, however, are best pursued through direct work experience. While most professional careers today require at least a bachelor's degree, not all do. There is still a place in our world for young people who want to embark on a career with nothing more than an entrepreneurial spirit and a willingness to work hard.

There are other reasons for getting a college education. It may be out of vogue these days, but there is still enormous value in getting a good liberal arts education—one that helps a young person become competent in subjects like history, philosophy, the humanities, art, science, literature, and languages. Much of higher education today is so specialized and pragmatic that students sometimes graduate without the ability to think deeply or to possess what has come to be known as *cultural literacy*. It's good to get a well-rounded education.

College is also a good place for students to meet and forge relationships with others their age who share their interests and dreams. Choice of college will often dictate the type of people they meet in the dormitories and lecture halls. A state university or "party school" will likely have a different social life than an Ivy League university or a Christian school. College is also where many young people will meet their future mates. Our older son met his bride while in college.

College may also provide your kids with their first opportunity to live away from home. When they have experienced the freedom of independent living for a few years, they are less likely to move back in with Mom and Dad when they graduate.

When students are away from home, they have a chance to grow up and to mature on their own without depending on their parents for everything. When kids go away to college, they suddenly realize they are on their own, that nobody's going to make them clean their dorm room, nobody's going to make them study, nobody's going to ask where they've been or what they're doing. Most college freshmen come to the realization sooner or later that they will need to become more disciplined. They'll decide to study not because someone told them to but because they want and need to. It's amazing how rapidly kids can mature when they are away at college. We've seen this happen with all three of our children. They leave for college as teenagers and return as young adults.

It's Expensive

A college education can be one of the most expensive purchases you will ever make. It can cost more than a new house. For that reason alone, decisions regarding college should not be taken lightly. If you or your student can't afford the tuition, room and board, and other expenses, your options are limited.

There are many ways to finance a college education, however—student loans, scholarships, financial aid, low cost junior colleges, and work-study programs. Nowadays almost anyone can go to college who really wants to. Many students assume their own college debts and carry them for many years.

If parents opt to fund their children's college expenses, it is normally done at great personal sacrifice. My wife and I look forward with great anticipation to that glorious day when our third and final college student graduates. *No more monthly tuition checks!*

Which brings up a thorny issue. If you pay for your children's college education, is it reasonable for you to expect them to perform at some minimum academic standards? The answer is yes. If you are paying the bills, the student should maintain a reasonable grade point average, take enough classes to graduate on time, and earn extra money to cover incidental or personal expenses. If they can't or won't perform at these standards, then you should withdraw your support. Let them choose other options such as a community college or getting a full-time job and living on their own.

The objective is not to micromanage your kids' lives or to control them while they are away from home. Students understandably resent their parents making their financial support contingent on academic performance, but if parents don't do this, they are actually violating the dignity and freedom of the student. To pay a student's way without strings attached only fosters a sense of parental dependency—not independence and self-reliance. This is an issue of responsibility, not parental control. A parent supporting a college student is in essence that student's employer. Every employer requires a certain level of performance or production before the employee is rewarded with a paycheck. In the same way, a certain level of performance should be required in exchange for a tuition check.

A Plug for Christian Colleges

Let me encourage you to consider a Christian college for your kids. All three of ours went to Christian schools, and not only did each one get a quality education, but they got it in a quality environment where faith is viewed in harmony, not conflict, with academics. In addition, your son or daughter will meet and build relationships with students and faculty members who will likely become friends and mentors for many years. For more information, contact the Coalition of Christian Colleges and Universities at http://www.cccu.org.

Put a Copilot
in Their Future

Young people who try to find the perfect mate never stop to ask themselves why someone perfect would ever be interested in them.

Most young people leave home to go away to college, to pursue a career, to join the military, or just to get away from their parents. Earlier in history, the only reason a young adult left home was to get married. That tradition goes all the way back to the Book of Genesis: "For this reason a man will leave his father and mother and be united to his wife" (2:24).

But today's youth aren't as anxious as their ancestors to get married right away. They typically postpone marriage until late into their twenties or even their thirties. The average age of marriage has steadily increased in recent years for a number of reasons, not the least of which is the rising divorce rate. Young people who have observed so many failed marriages—often including the marriage of their own parents—are less likely to marry early themselves. Some never marry at all.

That's why it's so important for parents to give their own marriages a high priority. As an earlier chapter stressed, the best gift you can give your kids is the example of a healthy marriage—one that lasts a lifetime. My family tree has been remarkably divorce-free compared to so many others, and for that I am grateful. It's a wonderful blessing to be able to pass on to your children a family tradition that includes a history of strong marriages.

Young people postpone marriage for other reasons too. Many wait until their education is finished. Some wait for economic reasons—they want to make sure they have a good job and some financial security. Some spend years looking for that "perfect" mate—as if such a person actually existed. Others just get so involved in their careers that they don't have time to get married or any desire to disrupt their selfish lifestyles.

Marriage and Dating

Your kids need to know that even though some marriages are not successful, theirs can be. No matter what has happened in their own family or to families that they know, marriage is still something they can look forward to with great anticipation. It was created and instituted by God as the basic foundation for the family unit, and it will never go out of style.

When your kids start dating seriously, they should understand that every dating relationship has the potential to end in marriage. Most won't, of course, but when young people have that perspective, they'll be more likely to treat those they date with greater discernment and respect. They'll have healthier dating relationships. The real purpose of dating is—to use an old-fashioned word—*courtship*. When I was growing up, I really don't think I wasted my time with girls I couldn't imagine myself marrying. Like most young people my age, I dated to have a good time and to be like everyone else. But I was also involved in that ancient ritual dance of courtship—wondering each time if she might be *the one*.

Another old-fashioned word that escapes many kids today is *romance*. You don't need soft violins and roses to be romantic (although they help), but you do need respect, courtesy, thoughtfulness, tenderness, and sometimes a little creativity. My nephew Justin recently proposed to his fiancée by kneeling in front of her with a pan of water and a towel. Gently washing her feet, he asked for her hand in marriage while vowing to love and serve her forever. Not bad for a young postmodern! Kids today can be romantic in their relationships if they have a high view of marriage and observe their own parents being romantic once in a while.

Go Ahead—Be a Matchmaker

You can't choose your son's or daughter's mate for them, but you can give them a healthy perspective on dating and marriage that will inspire them and

guide them in their relationships. You can also encourage them to look forward to that day when they will know they have found their future husband or wife.

If your son or daughter is seeing someone seriously, try not to interfere and don't be overly critical if you're not too fond of his or her partner. Hopefully you'll have an opportunity at some point to share any concerns you might have or to offer your encouragement. I'll never forget the day I was out working with my dad and half-jokingly and half-seriously he said to me, "Wayne, if I were you, I'd marry that girl Marci. I sure wouldn't let her get away." That's all it took. We were married the next year.

I was out fishing with my son Nate a few years ago when I said to him, half-jokingly and half-seriously, "Nate, if I were you, I'd marry that girl Tamara. I sure wouldn't let her get away." Trying to conceal the smile on his face, he began to express to me a wide range of concerns regarding money and job security. I assured him that he would probably do just fine. Most couples have to struggle the first few years to get on their feet. "If you really believe she's the one you want to spend the rest of your life with, I sure wouldn't let those mundane things get in my way." He and Tamara were married the next year.

You can't choose your kids' mates, but you'll probably play a big role in their marriage plans. Many young people end up choosing partners who are very much like their parents. Others choose mates who are quite the opposite, just to spite their parents. Kids will often model their marriages after what they have observed in their own family, for better or for worse.

I enjoy speaking to groups of teenagers on the subject of marriage and family. Being bullish on marriage, I love to challenge kids to imagine being married someday to that special person God has picked out for them. They may not know who it is, but God does. And it is His will for them to have a happy and long life together. Sometimes we stop and pray right there during the meeting for their future mates—wherever they are, whoever they might be—that God would protect and nurture them physically, intellectually, emotionally, and spiritually. Believe me, those kids do some serious praying.

Marriage isn't for everybody, of course. Your child may choose to remain single, and you should be supportive if he does. But by encouraging a healthy appreciation for marriage, we will make it easier for him to enter into a satisfying and rewarding marriage of his own. It's a wonderful thing to watch your son exchange wedding vows with your future daughter-in-law. And it's even more wonderful to become a grandparent!

Send Them on a Solo Flight

In order to become an experienced pilot, a person needs hundreds of hours of flying time.

Solo. On your own. Every pilot gets sweaty palms just thinking about his first solo flight . . . before and after it takes place. First, there are the lessons, with the flight instructor always at the ready to provide modeling, training, and rescue if necessary. But finally, when the time is right, the instructor gets out of the cockpit and says, "It's all yours." As most pilots will tell you, they usually have more problems dealing with their anticipation and fear of this event than they do actually flying the airplane.

There are many solo experiences in life. The first day at school, the first plunge into the deep end of the pool without water wings, the first overnight stay at camp, the first time driving a car, the first date, a first performance at church or in a class at school or on the athletic field. Like the young pilot who takes the plane up for that first short flight and returns safely, every solo experience during childhood and adolescence is a kind of dress rehearsal for the "big one"—when they finally leave home for good.

Every young person looks forward to the day when they'll have their independence, especially as they reach their midteen years. But there is also a natural fear of the unknown. They won't admit it, but it's there. They sometimes hide their anxiety and put it off for as long as possible. And because parents have fears of their own concerning their offspring's, as well as their own, preparedness for the big day, they are often reluctant to let go.

That's why it's a good idea to send your kids on a solo flight as soon as they are ready. In some ways the process is similar to the mother eagle that pushes her babies out of the nest for the first time. The young eaglet flaps his wings wildly and invariably does a rapid descent. But the mother eagle is not far away. Soaring above, she's there to swoop down if necessary and catch the little one before any serious harm is done. In the same way, we can give our kids opportunities to try out their wings. They may return to the nest for varying periods of time, but they will at least have experienced the exhilaration of flying solo.

Into the Wild Blue Yonder

With all three of our children, their first true solo flight took them away to college. We encouraged them to go away to college, preferably one that was far enough away from home to make it a true solo experience. That meant they couldn't come running home every time they needed something or got a little bit lonely.

Because college is not considered a permanent departure from home, it serves as an ideal rehearsal for independent living. Students who live in a dormitory learn very quickly that they must become responsible for themselves; there's no one around to make sure they get things done. College faculties refuse to serve as surrogate parents or baby-sitters.

If your son or daughter stays home while going to college, or if they don't go to college at all, then look for other opportunities for them to leave home, even if it's only for the summer.

Perhaps they could take a summer job working at a camp, or do short-term mission work for a month or two in a foreign country. They could find a job in another city, join the Peace Corps, or do a "mission year" of volunteer service like that required of Mormon students. Tony and Bart Campolo's Kingdomworks project in Philadelphia is an example of one program that provides opportunities for college-age students to spend a year serving God in the inner-city before making a decision about their career or college plans.

Regardless of when, where, or how it is done, a solo flight away from home will provide the physical distance necessary to allow young people to put some emotional distance between themselves and home. While this is not an easy thing to do, it is necessary and beneficial to everyone involved. Invariably, when the young person does return home, things will not be the same.

The Right Time

The timing, means, and circumstances of the first solo flight will vary with each young person. In all likelihood, the best time to start planning for it is during their junior or senior year of high school. Typically most kids are ready to go after graduation.

It's best however not to force your child to leave home. The decision to go should be jointly made by parents and kids. As parents, we want the leaving to be as smooth and as natural as possible. Timing is of great importance. Too early a push toward independence may cause young adults to "crash and burn," greatly damaging their self-confidence. A push too late usually results in increased conflict and a growing unhealthy dependence on parents.

Every person is different in terms of maturity, personality, experience, and needs. Like the flight instructor, a parent needs to carefully observe and evaluate when the window of opportunity opens. That's why it's important to look forward to that day, to get them ready, to give them permission to give it a shot, and sometimes to push (or nudge) them out of the nest.

Don't worry if your kids don't have it all together when they take their first solo flight. Most pilots don't. In order to become an experienced pilot, a person needs hundreds of hours of flying time before he is ready to fly in bad weather or at night. In due time, he will learn complex navigation procedures and instrument flying.

Your kids also need staging and phasing into independence, even though they have little experience in living on their own. It doesn't have to be an all-at-once, sink-or-swim proposition. Eventually, your children will gain the confidence and experience they need to truly fly on their own, as well as the ability to handle whatever life throws at them.

Say Good-Bye
and Let 'Em Fly!

Your job as a parent is to let the show go on as scheduled, without any further prompting from the wings.

Even though you may be looking forward with great anticipation to the day when your son or daughter leaves home, you'll probably have a tough time when it comes. Most parents do. Separation is never easy, even though kids have been separating from you since the instant they were born. When your kids first came into the world, they used all their strength and energy to separate from Mother's womb, a painful event for everyone involved. You've been confronting that pain ever since.

Now comes the final separation. Throughout this book, we've emphasized that adolescence is a time of preparation for adulthood, a great rehearsal for independence. There comes a time when—ready or not—the rehearsal is over and the performance must begin. Your job as a parent is to let the show go on as scheduled, without any further prompting from the wings.

Everyone leaves home a little differently. Some sneak away; some need to be pushed out or encouraged to go. Others are quite matter-of-fact about it all; they just clean out their room and they're gone. Even kids from the same family rarely depart in the same fashion. One may leave to go away to college. Another may leave to take a job away from home. Another may leave because of marriage. Another may leave to join the military. Some leave because of family problems such as abuse, escalating conflict, or a clash of values. Some leave only to return a few months or years later. Others leave

and rarely come home, even for visits. Some go far away; others stay close. Some leave when they are eighteen or younger, others much later.

Ideally, you want your son or daughter to leave at the right time for the right reasons; the details will vary from family to family and child to child. But you'll know when it comes. If you're ready and if your kids are ready, just like childbirth, it will be a time of joy and celebration for everyone involved as well as a time of some pain and struggle.

Flight Delays

Sometimes kids are ready to leave home, but their parents aren't ready for them to leave. Parents who deny or delay letting their kids go usually fall into one of six categories:

1. *Guilt-ridden parents.* They either waited too long to begin the process of preparing their kids, or they did nothing at all. They think they can make up for it by just letting their kids stay at home as long as they want.

2. *Perfectionistic parents.* They are disappointed in how their kids turned out. They think if they just have a little more time, they can do better. These parents often compare their kids with others their age who seem more mature or more capable, and they are afraid to let them go because they just aren't good enough.

3. *Distrustful parents.* They've witnessed too many crash-landings. They've seen their kids make major mistakes and poor choices. They don't want history to repeat itself, and lacking trust, they prevent their kids from leaving.

4. *Worried parents.* Some parents are paralyzed by fear—a fear of the unknown. Their inability to predict the future worries them. They can't imagine their kids surviving, let alone prospering, in such a hostile and complicated world.

5. *Angry parents.* When parents harbor feelings of hostility toward their children, they are often reluctant to let them go. Letting them go almost seems like a reward for bad behavior.

6. *Needy parents.* Many parents live their lives vicariously through their kids and their accomplishments. Their identity is wrapped up in being a parent. They may enjoy the authority they have as a parent. After all, it's hard to be the boss if you don't have anyone to boss around. They may enjoy their role as provider, and they need to have someone who is dependent on them for everything. They may fear the loneliness that will inevitably come when their kids are no longer around. Feelings like these can cause parents to delay their children's break from home for as long as possible.

Parents like these would be much better off just letting their kids go. While their reasons for hanging on are understandable, they aren't defensible. If their offspring do remain at home, there is little chance that the relationship they have with their parents will be a healthy one.

Leaving As a State of Mind

Releasing a child into adulthood, the final letting go, doesn't necessarily mean that your kids have to move out of the house. You can let go of your kids and officially declare them to be independent adults, even though they may be close by. This may involve their paying rent, sharing household expenses, or adding separate living quarters for them, such as a private bath or entrance from the outside. In these living arrangements, there still must be distance between parents and children, even if it's not geographic distance.

Decide on a Departure Date

Some parents mistakenly believe that their kids will leave home when they get good and ready. While there is some truth to that, it's best to be more intentional about it. If you just wait for it to happen, it might not. If it happens unexpectedly or abruptly, no one will have had time to prepare for it or accept it fully. That can be hard on both parents and their offspring. If kids don't have time to get ready, their chances for failure increase. Parents, too, need time to make the emotional adjustments that are required.

Decide on a date that is mutually acceptable to everyone. It could be tied to an event, such as a graduation from high school or college. It could be marriage, a job, or a birthday. Like the story Jesus told of the prodigal son, you might give your son or daughter an "inheritance," some seed money to jump-start their life away from home. Even if things don't work out exactly as planned, you will be working toward a departure date.

Put Some Thorns in the Nest

One of the reasons many young people today stay at home is because they have it made in the shade. Why start at the bottom when you can live at home comfortably for free? Whatever kids are, they aren't stupid. As long as Mom and Dad will provide a roof over their heads, do their laundry, cook their meals, pay their utilities, buy their gas, and let them have as much freedom as they want, why leave? That way, they can use their own money for fun stuff like going on ski trips or taking a European vacation.

That's why I recommend putting thorns in the nest. It's your nest, after all, and you have every right to make and enforce the house rules. Set limits on how much noise they can make. Make them do their share of the housework. Make them responsible for additional chores, or make them pay room

and board. Eventually they will come to the conclusion that it might be better to just get started on a life of their own.

Celebrate

On the day your kids do leave home, celebrate. Throw a party, fix their
favorite dinner, or pull out all your old family home videos and watch them
one more time together. Give them a blessing when they leave home. Let
your son know how proud you are of him and how confident you are that
he'll do well. I'll never forget the tears in my dad's eyes when he simply said,
"Thanks for being such a good son."

A mixture of conflicting emotions—anxiety and anticipation, sadness and
joy—invariably accompanies saying good-bye. When our son Nate pulled
out of our driveway with all his belongings in the back of his pickup truck,
my wife and I grinned and waved furiously until he was out of sight. Then
we just looked at each other and started to cry, which was something of a
relief to me as I was feeling a little guilty about being so happy.

Redecorate the Nest

It's time to move on . . .

When the last of our three kids left home, Marci and I looked around and realized that our home was a disaster area. Three teenagers living in your house over a span of about fifteen years will trash any home.

So we got busy and started redecorating. We turned Amber's bedroom into a guest room. By taking space out of Corey's bedroom, we added a walk-in closet to the master bedroom, and we were also able to enlarge the master bath. We replaced our carpets throughout the house. I've always wanted some of that nice thick white carpet that feels so good to walk on in bare feet. You can't have that kind of carpet with teenagers in the house. We repainted, replaced worn-out furniture, and bought a hot tub.

Besides increasing the size of our debt and improving the looks of our house, we accomplished some other things by redecorating. First, we resisted the temptation to turn our home into a museum. Some empty nesters offer tours of their home so you can see what it would have been like had their children actually cleaned their rooms. You see their children's beds, their old toys and sports equipment, their awards, pennants, and photos on the wall. Ugh. When we redecorated, we officially began the next phase of our lives.

Second, we sent a clear message to our kids that the next phase of *their* lives had officially begun. They were on their own. They no longer had bedrooms in our house. All their old stuff had either been discarded or stored in boxes in the attic. The old homeplace no longer looked the same. The new guest room was for guests. But all was not lost. Our children did qualify as guests, and we would always be happy to have them visit.

Getting On with Life

Nothing is the same when your kids leave home. Suddenly you have less laundry to do. There are fewer muddy footprints on your carpet. There's less loud music. The house is disturbingly quiet. There are fewer places at the dinner table. You have a hard time preparing meals for only two. Without students in the house, life loses its academic rhythm. Now you have to feed the dog, mow the lawn, do all the other chores. Your telephone bills skyrocket. If your kids are in college, your savings account balance plummets. You no longer have a reason to go to an amusement park. There's no longer a reason to close your bedroom door.

So how do you adjust to all these changes? Redecorating the house helps. But maybe it's equally important to redecorate or reinvent yourself a little bit. Who are you? How do you relate to your kids now? What is your new role? Friend? Interested party? Relative once removed? There are all kinds of emotions and issues that can surface when your kids leave home. Here are just few of them:

1. *A sense of joy.* If you have prepared yourself and your kids for their eventual departure, you will have no regrets when they leave home. Instead, you'll be proud of them and anxious to see what the next phase of life brings to you and them.

2. *A sense of sorrow and loss.* It's perfectly normal and expected to feel some pain. It's not easy to say good-bye to a child who has been part of your life for so many years, as well as his or her friends and the general household activity. And as with other kinds of loss, many emotions are aroused: sadness, relief, worry (Will he do okay?), anger (She never calls.), guilt (Why didn't I spend more time with him?).

3. *A role change.* Many parents have a tough time dealing with what often feels like a slow, disagreeable push into irrelevance. This is especially intense for those who have made parenting their full-time occupation.

4. *A confrontation with aging.* Having grown children is a clear marker of middle age. You may find yourself starting to count the number of years you have left. Some parents even feel envy as they watch their kids leave with their whole lives in front of them.

5. *A change in the marital relationship.* Husbands and wives become a twosome again for the first time in many years. This can bring with it new freedom and romance, but it also removes the distractions that may have masked problems in the relationship during the child-rearing years.

It's always best to anticipate and deal openly with issues such as these, to talk them over with your spouse, or to get advice from other parents who have gone through the same experience and survived. There are no Lamaze classes for this new stage of life, but you can talk to others who understand what you are going through.

Remember that your role as a parent has now moved to the stage of caring.

You can let your kids know you care by staying in touch with them in new ways, through letters, occasional care packages, words of encouragement that express confidence in them, and daily prayers.

It's now time to move on. Take inventory of other roles you play and pursue those things. What dreams did you put on hold in order to raise kids? What would you like to accomplish during the next half of your life? Maybe it's time to reinvent yourself.

And maybe it's also time to revisit the relationship you and your spouse had before you became parents. Be romantic again. Put some sizzle back in the marriage and have some fun.

Now that we've redecorated, Marci and I love our empty nest. I think you'll enjoy yours too.

Stay Out of
Their Airspace

"Billy, I just don't know if you'll ever amount to anything."
"Dad, please. I'm seventy years old. I'm an old man. Give it up!"

Some parents just never stop parenting. They live by the motto "A parent's job is never done."

But there comes a time when every parent must let go and let their kids live their own lives without interference. And for most, it's sooner than they think.

Parents frequently ask me what they can do about a twenty-year-old son or daughter who is involved in something they don't approve of. I tell them there is very little they can do. "By the time your kids reach their eighteenth or nineteenth birthday," I tell them, "for all intents and purposes, you're done. There's very little that you can do to influence their behavior now."

That doesn't mean that people don't or won't change after they reach young adulthood. It only means that they must do it on their own. If your kids haven't learned what they need to learn from you by the time they reach legal adulthood, they won't learn it from you now. They will likely recall much of what you taught them (which is why so many young adults suddenly realize that their parents weren't as stupid as they thought), but you must back off.

Unhealthy Parental Roles

When your kids leave home, you'll need to develop a new mind-set concerning your parental role. This will require a good deal of faith and trust—both in your children and in the faithfulness of God.

211

To let go successfully, it's helpful to be aware of some of the unhealthy roles that parents often play in the lives of their departing offspring.

- *The Meddler.* This is the parent who calls their adult children constantly, visits excessively, asks endless and detailed questions about their lives. This may be a parent's way of expressing genuine interest and concern, but to newly independent young adults it is usually interpreted as prying or snooping.
- *The Manipulator.* This is the parent who tries to control their children's behavior with anger, bribery, guilt, or any number of other tactics. "After all we've done for you, how could you treat us this way?"
- *The Critic.* This is the parent who can't resist offering an opinion on everything their son or daughter does. Some adult children feel like they are always under a microscope, always being judged by their parents. And most of the time, they know they will never quite measure up.
- *The Stranger.* This is the parent who seems to abandon their adult children. While we need to let go, we must never communicate to our kids that we have abandoned our love and concern for them. Even grownups need to know that their parents will be there for them, especially in difficult times.

A Healthy Parental Relationship

You really can look forward to your children leaving the nest. That's not only true because you'll have a bedroom that can be turned into an office or a home gym, but also because you will enjoy a wonderful new kind of relationship with them. That is really the payoff for all your hard work and sacrifice. It is truly rewarding to be able to communicate with your kids on a whole new level of understanding and to feel the old parent-child gap beginning to close.

If you want to establish and maintain a good relationship with your airborne kids, then find ways to give your kids the following:

- *Your trust.* Let them know that you have faith in them and their ability to succeed.

- *Your respect*. They need to be treated the same as you would treat any other adult. This means giving them privacy, space, and courtesy. It means asking, not assuming what they want or need, not treating them rudely, not making demands on them just because they are your kids, not criticizing everything they do.
- *Your friendship*. You'll never stop being their parent, but you can also be their friend. You can have good times together, laugh and joke and cry together. You can do with your kids what you do with your friends: go to movies, go out to eat, go shopping, go on a camping trip.
- *Your admiration*. Kids never stop wanting affirmation from their parents. No matter how old you get, you never stop wanting to hear your parents brag on you to friends and relatives. Let your adult kids know that you are proud of them and what they've become.
- *Your caring*. This is the fifth and final stage of parenting. Caring involves giving adult children plenty of freedom to live their lives apart from us, while communicating at the same time that we care deeply about them. Kids need to know that they can depend on us when they truly need our help and our prayers.
- *Your love*. Above all, your children need to know that you love them deeply. And like the love that comes from our heavenly Father, it should be a love that is without end. Our adult kids need affection from us expressed in hugs, kisses, and words. They will value our treating them with respect and courtesy.

Be Patient with Homing Pigeons

They're baaaaack!

Your nest is empty. The kids are gone. The house is nice and tidy. You are enjoying peace and quiet. Life is good.

Then, without warning, there's a knock at the door. It's your grown offspring with all of his belongings—not there for a visit, but to stay.

How do you handle "boomerang kids"? What will you do when your fully grown, independent offspring pops back into your nest? This is not an uncommon problem for parents these days. More and more young people are finishing college, running out of money, and returning home. It's hard not to take them in. You can't just tell them to go away, can you?

According to researchers, more than 60 percent of eighteen- to twenty-four-year-olds live with their parents or depend on them financially today compared with only 40 percent in 1960. Some adult children don't leave home until middle age. Close to 15 percent of twenty-five- to thirty-four-year-olds live with their parents.

Home from College

There are a variety of reasons why adult children return home.

If your son or daughter is a college student who has lived in a dorm all year, he or she will probably come home during breaks and summer vacation. For a student who has lived away from home for a good part of the year, moving back home can be very strange.

When our son Corey came home the summer after his freshman year, we were of course happy to see him. We had a very positive first week while he was home. Things went downhill fast after that. Corey had become accustomed to living under his own set of house rules, and he wasn't about to start living by ours again.

We experienced quite a bit of conflict that summer. Succeeding years got progressively better, and we enjoyed his summer visits. He got a good summer job that kept him busy, he willingly accepted his share of the household duties, and avoided conflict. He matured quite a bit in college.

When your kids return home, even for a short time, you are forced to make adjustments. Many of your normal routines are disrupted. Kids come and go at all hours. The house gets messy again. Most of the phone calls aren't for you. You feel guilty making him watch the news program that you always watch on Tuesday night.

When college students return home, it can be difficult. Even though you have the same house rules you have always had, things won't be the same. Your son or daughter will have had a taste of freedom and won't go back to being a child again.

Home to Stay

But sometimes young adults return home with the intention of staying for an indefinite period of time. Perhaps they failed or dropped out of college. They may have had employment or financial problems. There may have been marriage problems—a divorce or abandonment. Some young people come home because of substance-abuse problems, emotional problems, health problems, a refusal to accept responsibility, or even homesickness.

It's not uncommon for some young people to demand their freedom when they are eighteen, only to return a few years later completely changed, ready to abide by the rules, and suddenly grateful for a nice place to live and such wonderful parents to take care of them.

In most cases, kids return home only temporarily until they can find a new job, new housing, or make a decision about where they want to go or what they want to do. Quite often such visitations by your kids can actually be quite positive and enriching to your lives. It's nice to have your kids come home—for a little while. Short-term, transitional returns don't need to be difficult. They rarely last long; everyone cooperates and knows that there's an end in sight.

If your adult offspring comes home to stay, things can get difficult indeed. Sometimes they return disillusioned, broke, in serious trouble, or perhaps with small children in tow. In situations like these, you need to understand what your new role will be and how to handle living arrangements so that everyone will survive.

New Rules

While you shouldn't ignore problems, the last thing returning offspring need from their parents at this stage is recrimination and advice—at least not at first. They know what's wrong without your telling them. Acceptance and love should come first, not punishment and lecturing.

Nor should you rescue. You may be tempted to fix their situation immediately by paying their bills or bailing them out of whatever problem they are in. That urge should also be resisted. You can offer them a place of temporary sanctuary, but don't deny them their independence and self-respect. As much as they would like for you to solve their problems for them, you can't. Empathize and help them find a way out on their own.

While they are living with you, think of them as guests in your home—visiting adults rather than returning children. If their stay is a long one, then think of them as boarders.

Clarify expectations and apprehensions ahead of time. Don't wait for problems to arise. Talk about the situation before they actually move their stuff in. Agree on specific issues ahead of time. Be frank, honest, open. Discuss worries, potential problems, and how you might deal with them before, not after, the fact.

Above all, don't let your returning adult children forget that it's your home, not theirs. Make it clear that they must abide by your rules while they are under your roof. They should be the ones who are inconvenienced—not you.

Here are some things to consider:

- *Phone rules*. If they want a phone for social calls, they can pay for their own phone line. No long-distance calls without permission.

- *Noise rules*. Set limits on parties, friends who visit, TV and computer use, and volume of music. You have become accustomed to peace and quiet. You need to discuss what your needs are and make sure they comply with these limits—or move out.
- *Transportation rules*. Does he have a car of his own? If he uses yours, what about gas, upkeep, insurance, and other expenses?
- *Schedule rules*. What about mealtimes? Will you eat together, or is everybody on their own? Older youth like to stay up until the wee hours, but perhaps you don't like being disturbed after eleven. Discuss this and establish rules.
- *Lifestyle rules*. If your grown children have adopted behavior that you don't approve of—smoking, drinking, or pornography—make sure they understand that these behaviors are not permitted in your home.
- *Money rules*. Charge your live-at-home kids for room and board. If they are unemployed, demand household services in lieu of rent. Be clear and firm that they either pay up or find another place to live. They may just find it easier to do the latter.

While things are never the same when your kids come home, it's still important for you to continue to lead your own life. Don't change your schedule to accommodate theirs. Don't worry about where they are or what they are doing. Don't worry about keeping them entertained, happy, well fed, or properly clothed. They will actually be better off knowing that they aren't intruding on your normal schedule.

If possible, give your returning young adults some privacy. Try to give them separate living quarters or at least a place where they can get away from you. One couple put a chair, lamp, and TV set in their tiny laundry room just so their prodigal son could have his own place to relax and retreat.

Insist that they get jobs and support themselves. Decide whether that artist offspring of yours is really a deadbeat. You may need to find some way to convince her that her passion for saving the whales is best pursued as a hobby rather than a career.

Don't give your son or daughter serious amounts of money without demanding something in return. Set up a loan through a bank or some other financial institution, and make them pay interest, monthly payments, the whole bit.

Silver Lining

Ideally, you want your kids to have the ability to make it on their own. If they do return, however, keep in mind that it's not all bad news. There are some benefits and joys to go along with the difficulties.

For example, not all parents get a second chance to work on the relationship they have with their offspring. Perhaps you need to explore new ways of communicating with each other or new ways of forgiving each other. This can be a time of real healing and reconciliation.

Living together again can give your kids a chance to see you in a different light. It's amazing what your kids miss when they are at home the first time. You may have a new opportunity to mentor your kids, to continue your influence in their lives.

Having kids at home also provides another opportunity to bless your kids. You can give them some much-needed affirmation and encouragement that they might not get anywhere else. You can listen to them and pray with them.

You may find also that it makes good sense to have your son or daughter living with you as a young adult. It can be a win-win situation for both of you financially if you are sharing living expenses. If you enjoy being together and are good at keeping each other company, it's possible to "leave the nest" without actually leaving the nest!

Like the father of the prodigal son, we should be able to welcome our kids home with open arms of comfort, acceptance, and forgiveness. We may not be able to kill the fatted calf and have a party, but we can at least give them the kind of love that only parents can provide. This is the first step toward the healing and restoration that will need to take place in their lives.

Let Them Complete the Journey on Their Own

All you can do is give them wings . . .

Y ou're done.

Your offspring has flown away. They are fully grown. On their own. Sure, you keep them on your radar screen and make contact from time to time, but basically they are up, up and away. They don't need you in the same ways as before.

Not that they are so mature and so capable that they won't lose their bearings, fly into bad weather, or even experience a few crash-landings. But hopefully they know enough to keep those things from being fatal. They'll survive.

As parents, we can only take our kids so far. We can get them in the air, but they are a long way from being finished as human beings. They still have a lot of growing up to do.

But don't we all? Are you finished yet? I know I'm not. I'm still a work in progress.

Don't feel guilty if when your kids leave home, they don't seem to have it all together yet. We just have to trust that eighteen years or so is all that's needed from us. From that point on, your son or daughter should have enough experience and enough maturity and enough intelligence to figure the rest out on his or her own. All you can do is give them wings.

Nobody does a perfect job of raising children to adulthood. Nobody. Your parents didn't, and mine didn't either. I didn't, and you won't. But raising children to be responsible adults is about trusting God, the only One who is truly capable of being the perfect parent. Trust that even though you weren't able to finish the job, He will. He "who began a good work in you [and your kids!] will carry it on to completion until the day of Christ Jesus" (Philippians 1:6).

Sources and
Recommended Reading

Anderson, Herbert, and Kenneth Mitchell. *Leaving Home*. Louisville, Ky.: Westminster/John Knox Press, 1993.

Baldwin, Bruce. *Beyond the Cornucopia Kids*. Wilmington, N.C.: Direction Dynamics, 1988.

Beausay, Bill. *Shaping the Man Inside Teenage Boys: Surviving and Enjoying These Extraordinary Years*. Colorado Springs: Waterbrook Press, 1998.

Black, Thom. *Kicking Your Kid Out of the Nest*. Grand Rapids: Zondervan Publishing House, 1996.

Brain, Marshall. *The Teenager's Guide to the Real World: How to Become a Successful Adult*. BYG Publishing, P.O. Box 40492, Raleigh, N.C. 27629, 1997.

Drescher, John. *If I Were Starting My Family Again*. Nashville: Abingdon, 1979.

Elkind, David. *All Grown Up and No Place to Go*. Reading, Mass.: Addison-Wesley, 1984.

Elkind, David. *Parenting Your Teenager*. New York: Ballantine Books, 1993.

Elkind, David. *Ties That Stress*. Cambridge, Mass.: Harvard University Press, 1994.

Feeney, Rik. *So You Want to Move Out? A Guide to Living on Your Own*. Richardson Publishing, 1007 E. Main St., Albemarle, N.C. 28001, 1994.

Garbarino, James. *Raising Children in a Socially Toxic Environment*. San Francisco: Jossey-Bass Publishers, 1995.

Glenn, H. Stephen, and Jane Nelson. *Raising Self-Reliant Children in a Self-Indulgent World*. Rocklin, Calif.: Prima Publishing, 1989.

Greene, Lawrence. *The Life-Smart Kid*. Rocklin, Calif.: Prima Publishing, 1995.

Groseclose, Kel. *This Too Shall Pass*. Nashville: Dimensions for Living, 1995.

Habermas, Ron. *Raising Teenagers While They're Still in Pre-School*. Joplin, Mo.: College Press, 1998.

Hancock, Jim. *Raising Adults: Getting Kids Ready for the Real World*. Colorado Springs: Piñon, 1999.

Hine, Thomas. *The Rise and Fall of the American Teenager*. New York: Avon Books, 1999.

Holleman, Joan, and Audrey Sherins. *How to Embarass Your Kids without Even Trying*.

Joy, Donald. *Sex, Strength and the Secrets of Becoming a Man.* Ventura, Calif.: Regal Books, 1990.

Kesler, Jay. *Emotionally Healthy Teenagers.* Nashville: Word Books, 1998.

Kuykendall, Carol. *Give Them Wings: Preparing for the Time Your Teen Leaves Home.* Colorado Springs: Focus on the Family, 1994.

Lewis, Robert. *Raising a Modern Day Knight.* Colorado Springs: Focus on the Family, 1996.

Lewis, Vern, and Bruce Narramore. *Cutting the Cord: The Adventure of Leading Your Child Through Adolescence.* Wheaton, Ill.: Tyndale House, 1990.

Littwin, Susan. *The Postponed Generation: Why American Youth Are Growing Up Later.* New York: William Morrow and Co., 1986.

MacKenzie, Robert J. *Setting Limits: How to Raise Responsible, Independent Children by Providing Reasonable Boundaries.* Rocklin, Calif.: Prima Publishing, 1993.

Mahdi, Louise Carus, Nancy Geyer Christopher, and Michael Meade. eds. *Crossroads: The Quest for Contemporary Rites of Passage.* Chicago and LaSalle, Ill.: Open Court, 1996.

Maxwell, John. *Breakthrough Parenting.* Colorado Springs: Focus on the Family, 1996.

McPherson, Miles. *The Power of Believing in Your Child.* Minneapolis: Bethany House, 1998.

Minear, Dr. Ralph E., and William Proctor. *Kids Who Have Too Much.* Nashville: Thomas Nelson, 1989.

Mueller, Walt. *Understanding Today's Youth Culture, Rev. and ex.* Wheaton, Ill.: Tyndale House, 1998.

Nelson, Jane and Lynn Lott. *Positive Discipline for Teenagers.* Rocklin, Calif.: Prima Publishing, 1994.

Prager, Dennis. *Happiness Is a Serious Problem.* New York: Regan Book, 1998.

Rice, Wayne and David Veerman. *Understanding Your Teenager.* Nashville: Word Books, 1999.

Rosemond, John. *Ending the Homework Hassle.* Kansas City, Mo.: Andrews and McMeel, 1990.

Rosemond, John. *John Rosemond's Six Point Plan for Raising Happy, Healthy Children.* Kansas City, Mo.: Andrews and McMeel, 1989.

Rosemond, John. *Teen Proofing: A Revolutionary Approach to Fostering Responsible Decision Making in Your Teenager.* Kansas City, Mo.: Andrews and McMeel, 1998.

Saminow, Stanton. *Before It's Too Late.* New York: Times Books, 1989.

Sanders, Bill. *Seize the Moment, Not Your Teen.* Wheaton, Ill.: Tyndale House, 1997.

Schneider, Barbara, and David Stevenson. *The Ambitious Generation: America's Teenagers, Motivated but Directionless.* New Haven and London: Yale University Press, 1999.

Steede, Kevin. *10 Most Common Mistakes Good Parents Make.* Rocklin, Calif.: Prima Publishing, 1998.

Tapscott, Don. *Growing Up Digital: The Rise of the Net Generation.* New York: McGraw-Hill, 1998.

Veerman, Dave. *Ozzie and Harriet Had a Scriptwriter.* Wheaton, Ill.: Tyndale House, 1996.

Veerman, Dave. *Parenting Passages: Eleven Critical Experiences Every Parent Faces and How to Navigate Them.* Wheaton, Ill.: Tyndale House, 1994

White, Jerry and Mary. *When Your Kids Aren't Kids Anymore: Parenting Late-Teen and Adult Children.* Colorado Springs: NavPress, 1989.

Wilmes, David. *Parenting for Prevention: How to Raise a Child to Say No to Alcohol/Drugs.* Minneapolis: Johnson Institute, 1988.

Winkler, Kathleen. *College Bound.* St. Louis, Mo.: Concordia Publishing House, 1998.

Winn, Marie. *Children Without Childhood.* New York: Penguin Books, 1981.